THE KRINAR EXPOSÉ

A Krinar Chronicles Novel

ANNA ZAIRES & HETTIE IVERS

♠ Mozaika Publications ♠

This is a work of fiction. Names, characters, places, and incidents are either the product of the author's imagination or are used fictitiously, and any resemblance to actual persons, living or dead, business establishments, events, or locales is purely coincidental.

Copyright © 2018 Anna Zaires and Dima Zales
www.annazaires.com

All rights reserved.

Except for use in a review, no part of this book may be reproduced, scanned, or distributed in any printed or electronic form without permission.

Published by Mozaika Publications, an imprint of Mozaika LLC.
www.mozaikallc.com

Cover by Najla Qamber Designs
www.najlaqamberdesigns.com
Photo by Lindee Robinson Photography

e-ISBN: 978-1-63142-378-9
Print ISBN: 978-1-63142-407-6

Part One

THE X-CLUB

CHAPTER ONE

Two years since the invasion.

I couldn't believe it had been two years since the invasion, and we still knew next to nothing about the aliens who had taken over Earth.

Frustrated, I removed my glasses and rubbed my eyes, feeling the strain from staring at the computer screen all day. Over the past two weeks, ever since I'd decided to prove myself by writing an insightful piece about the invaders, I'd pored over every bit of information available on the internet, and all I had were rumors, a number of unreliable eyewitness accounts, some grainy YouTube videos, and as many unanswered questions as before.

Two years after K-Day, and the Ks—or the Krinar, as they liked to be called—were nearly as much of a mystery as when they'd first arrived.

My computer pinged, distracting me from my thoughts. Glancing at the screen, I saw that it was an email from my editor. Richard Gable wanted to know when I'd have the article on conjoined puppy twins ready for him.

At least it wasn't another one of those "sky is falling" emails from my mom.

Sighing, I rubbed my eyes again, pushing away distracting thoughts about my insane parents. It was bad enough my career still hadn't taken off. I had no idea why all the fluff pieces landed on my desk. It had been that way ever since I'd joined the newspaper three years ago, and I was sick and tired of it. At twenty-four years of age, I had about as much experience writing about real news as a college intern.

Fuck it, I'd decided last month. If Gable didn't want to assign me real work, I'd find a story myself. And what could be more interesting or controversial than the mysterious beings who'd invaded Earth and now resided alongside humans? If I could uncover something—anything—factual about the Ks, that would go a long way toward proving that I was capable of handling bigger stories.

Putting my glasses back on, I quickly wrote an email to Gable, requesting a couple of extra days to finish the puppy article. My excuse was that I wanted to interview the veterinarian and was having trouble getting in touch with him. It was a lie, of course—I'd interviewed both the veterinarian and the owner as soon as I got the assignment—but I wanted to avoid getting another fluff piece for a few days. It would give me time to explore an interesting topic I came across in my research today: the so-called x-clubs.

"Hey there, baby girl, any plans for tonight?"

I looked up at the familiar voice and grinned at Jay, my coworker and best friend, who'd just stepped into my tiny office. "Nope," I said cheerfully. "Going to catch up on some work and then veg out on my couch."

He sighed dramatically and gave me a look of mock reproof. "Amy, Amy, Amy… What are we going to do with you? It's Friday night, and you're going to stay in?"

"I'm still recovering from last weekend," I said, my grin widening. "So don't think you can drag me out again so soon. One night of Jay-style partying a month is plenty for me."

Jay-style partying was a unique experience consisting of multiple vodka shots early in the evening, followed by several hours of club-hopping and a dinner/breakfast at a twenty-four-hour Korean diner. I wasn't lying when I said I was still recovering—the combination of vodka and Korean food had given me a hangover that was more like a bad case of food poisoning. I'd barely crawled out of bed on Monday to go to work.

"Oh, come on," he cajoled, his brown eyes resembling those of a puppy. With his thick lashes, curly brown hair, and fine features, Jay was almost too pretty for a guy. If it hadn't been for his muscular build, he would've seemed effeminate. As it was, however, he attracted women and men alike —and enjoyed both with equal gusto.

"Sorry, Jay. Another week perhaps." What I needed to concentrate on now was my article about the Ks… and the secretive clubs they supposedly patronized.

Jay let out another sigh. "All right, have it your way. What are you working on right now? The puppy piece?"

I hesitated. I hadn't told Jay about my project yet, mostly because I didn't want to appear foolish if I couldn't come up with a good story. Jay didn't get a lot of meaty assignments either, but he didn't mind it as much as I did. His goal in life was to enjoy himself, and everything else—his journalism career included—came second. He thought ambition was something that was only useful in moderation and didn't apply himself more than necessary.

"I just don't want to be a total bum—for my parents, you know," he'd explained to me once, and that statement perfectly summed up his approach to work.

I, on the other hand, wanted more than to not be a bum. It bothered me that the editor had taken one look at my strawberry-blond hair and doll-like features and had permanently slotted me into fluff-piece land. I would've thought Gable was sexist, except he'd done the same thing to Jay. Our editor didn't discriminate against women; he just made assumptions about people's capabilities based on their looks.

Deciding to finally confide in my friend, I said, "No, not the puppy piece. I've actually been researching a project of my own."

Jay's perfectly shaped eyebrows rose. "Oh?"

"Have you ever heard of x-clubs?" I cast a quick look around to make sure we wouldn't be overheard. Thankfully, the offices around mine were largely empty, with only an intern working on the other side of the floor. It was nearly four p.m. on a Friday, and most people had found an excuse to leave early this summer afternoon.

Jay's eyes widened. "X-clubs? As in, xeno-clubs?"

"Yes." My heartbeat sped up. "Have you heard of them?"

"Aren't they the places those alien-crazy people go to hook up with Ks?"

"Apparently." I grinned at him. "I just learned

about them today. Do you know anyone who's been to one?"

Jay frowned, an expression that looked out of place on his normally cheerful face. "No, not really. I mean, there's always that 'friend of a friend of a friend,' but no one I know personally."

I nodded. "Right. And you know half of Manhattan, so these clubs, if they exist, are a closely guarded secret. Can you imagine the story?" In my best broadcaster's voice, I announced dramatically, "Alien clubs in the heart of New York City? *The New York Herald* brings you the latest in K news!"

"Are you sure about this?" My friend looked doubtful. "I've heard those clubs are near K Centers. Are you saying there are some in New York City?"

"I think so. There's some chatter online about a club in Manhattan. I want to find it and see what it's all about."

"Amy... I don't know if that's such a great idea." To my surprise, Jay appeared more disturbed than excited, his uncharacteristic frown deepening. "You don't want to mess with the Ks."

"Nobody wants to mess with them—which is why we still know nothing about them." My earlier frustration returned. It bothered me that everybody was still so intimidated by the invaders. "All I want to do is write a factual article about them. Specifically, about some places they allegedly frequent. Surely that's allowed. We still have freedom of press in this country, don't we?"

"Maybe," Jay said. "Or maybe not. Personally, I think they erase whatever information they don't want to be public. Used to be, once it's on the internet, it's there forever, but not anymore."

"You think they might suppress my article somehow?" I asked worriedly, and Jay shrugged.

"I have no idea, but if I were you, I'd focus on the puppy piece and forget about the Ks."

⁓

It was almost eight in the evening by the time I came across it: a mention of the x-club's location on an obscure online sex forum. It was buried within someone's lengthy—and rather improbable-sounding—account of his hook-up with a group of Ks. The feeling of ecstasy the man described sounded suspiciously like a drug-induced high to me, though similar tales littered the web, giving rise to all sorts of rumors about the invaders… including that of vampirism.

I didn't buy it, but then again, thanks to my mom's obsession with wacky conspiracy theories, I had a natural distrust of rumors. I liked facts; that's why I'd gone into journalism rather than choosing to write fiction.

According to this man's account, he had gone to the club right after his dinner in the Meatpacking District. He named the restaurant where he'd had dinner, and then he wrote that the club was directly across the street from it.

And just like that, I had a lead.

Jumping to my feet, I grabbed my bag and hurried out of the office, nodding to the janitor on the way.

It looked like my Friday night was about to get a lot more exciting.

CHAPTER TWO

"You don't have to come with me," I repeated for the fifth time, giving Jay an exasperated look. I'd made the mistake of texting him about my plans, and he'd showed up on my doorstep twenty minutes later, dressed for clubbing but doing his best to dissuade me from going.

"If you're going, I'm going," he said stubbornly. "I don't think either one of us should be doing this, but baby girl, you're crazy if you think I'll let you go there by yourself."

"You just want your name to be on the story," I joked, flipping my shoulder-length hair upside down to work in some mousse. My reddish-blond strands were naturally fine and straight, but if I put enough product in them, I could achieve some sexy waves. Sexy wasn't a look I normally tried for, but in this case, it was important. The Ks were not only humanoid in appearance, but downright gorgeous… and according to what I'd read online, they liked their human sex partners to be nearly as good-looking as they were.

I was fairly certain I didn't fit that criteria, but I was hoping that with enough makeup—and with contacts instead of glasses—I'd look pretty enough to be allowed into the club.

"Our names will *be* the story," Jay said darkly. "I can see it now: *Two Missing Journalists, Last Seen Hunting Aliens in Meatpacking District.*"

"Oh, please." I straightened and began applying mascara to my long brown lashes. "Since when are you afraid to go to a club? You do crazy stuff all the time—"

"Yes, but I do it for fun, not to prove myself to our idiot boss. And no amount of drinking or partying compares to trying to infiltrate an alien sex club. You do see the difference between a little recreational weed and this, don't you?"

"Yeah, yeah," I muttered, swiping blush onto my pale cheeks. "Like I told you, I only texted you about this so someone would know where I am. You don't have to come with me."

"Yes, I do." Jay gave me a "get real" look. "You're my only female friend. You think I'd let you get spirited away on some spaceship?"

"They live in K Centers on Earth, silly." I grinned at him in the mirror. "Why would they take me on a spaceship?"

"Who knows?" he said, plopping down on my couch. "Maybe they like cute, green-eyed blondes who wear glasses to work to seem smarter."

"Mmm, yes. I'm just their type." Laughing, I smoothed my hands down my blue, form-fitting dress. With my curvy hips, I wasn't exactly model material, though I was generally happy with my figure. It helped that my ex-boyfriends seemed to enjoy a rounder ass; one of them even claimed it was his favorite part of my body.

"You never know," Jay insisted. "Seriously, Amy, I wish you'd reconsider. Do you realize that they can do absolutely anything to you in that club, and nobody would stop them? Our laws don't apply to them. They can kill you, and nobody would blink an eye, treaty or no treaty. You understand that, right?"

"Of course I do." I was beginning to get tired of this conversation. Sometimes Jay could be like a dog with a bone. "I wasn't born yesterday. I know how dangerous the Ks can be. I've seen those videos of them ripping people to shreds, and I've read the eyewitness accounts. But we're journalists. We're supposed to investigate stories, to uncover important truths and bring them to light, even if there's risk involved. We didn't choose this profession so we could be writing about puppy twins or socialite weddings or whatever bullshit Gable assigns us. We need to be doing real reporting, Jay—and this is our chance."

Pausing, I gave him a level look. "I'm doing this—and you can either join me or go home."

CHAPTER THREE

"Okay, this is the restaurant," I said when our cab pulled up in front of a fancy-looking hotel. According to Google, the restaurant was on the rooftop of the building. "Now what?"

"Now we go to some real nightclubs and forget this insanity," Jay said, climbing out of the cab and opening the door for me. "You're already dressed up; it'll be perfect. We'll have a blast, just like last weekend."

I blew out an exasperated breath. "I'm not repeating last weekend for a good long time. I already told you that. And we're not here to party; we're here to observe."

"Right, of course." Jay sounded morose. "We're just going to quietly observe some aliens—who won't mind at all that we want to publicize their secrets."

I ignored him, trying to figure out where the club "across the street" could be. All around me, the area swarmed with beautiful people. Meatpacking was *the* clubbing district of Manhattan. Models, celebrities, Wall Streeters, and everyone else mingled on the cobblestone streets and in edgy-looking club-lounges, trying to outdo each other with designer bags and clothing. Music blared out of several open doorways, and drunk girls stumbled around in sky-high heels, giggling and flirting with every guy in sight.

I had to admit that the Ks were smart to locate their club here; with all the glittering crowds, even a Krinar could go unnoticed.

Studying the building across the street, I saw a group of tall, leggy women approaching an unassuming brown door. There was no sign above it, nothing to indicate what kind of establishment it was. One of the women knocked, and the door swung open, letting the group in. Then the door closed immediately.

My story-sniffing instincts went on full alert. "There," I said, grabbing Jay's arm and practically towing him across the busy street.

"How do you know?" His voice held an undertone of anxiety. "Did you see one of them?"

"No." I ignored the honking of cabs as I cut in front of several cars. "But I think I saw some women who might be their types."

"Their types?"

"Krinar-like," I explained, weaving through the crowds on the sidewalk. "Tall, gorgeous… like supermodels."

"That doesn't mean anything—"

"Look, let's just try this and see," I interrupted, stopping in front of the brown door. Turning toward Jay, I said, "Ready?"

"No," he said glumly, but I was already knocking on the door.

For a few seconds, nothing happened. Then the door quietly opened, revealing a narrow hallway.

"Okay, here we go," I whispered to Jay, and stepped inside.

He followed me in without another word.

As we walked silently through the hallway, I could feel my heartbeat picking up. Was it possible I would actually get to meet them in person? The invaders I'd only seen on TV?

The hallway ended in front of another door—this one metallic gray in color. It was locked, so I knocked again, not knowing what else to do.

Then I waited.

And waited.

And waited.

"I don't think they're going to let us in," Jay whispered after a minute. "Maybe we should leave."

"Not yet," I whispered back. I didn't want to admit it, but now that we were here, I was starting to get nervous as well. The full enormity of what we were doing was beginning to dawn on me. If this was indeed the x-club I'd heard about, then on the other side of that door were beings from another planet—from an ancient civilization that had supposedly seeded life on Earth.

My heart was now throbbing in my throat.

Gathering my courage, I knocked again and called out, "Hello?"

Jay gulped audibly next to me, his face turning pale.

"Hello?" I called out again, louder this time. Nervous or not, I wasn't leaving until I gave this my best shot.

"Amy, let's go—"

The door quietly slid open.

A man stood there, his tall, broad-shouldered frame taking up most of the doorway. In the low light, all I could see of his face were high cheekbones and a jaw that looked like it had been carved from granite. His eyes glittered darkly underneath thick eyebrows, and his clothes were pale, almost white.

Stunned, I stared at him. Could it be...? Could he be...?

The man smiled, his teeth flashing white in his bronzed face. "Welcome," he said softly, and stepped aside, motioning for us to come in.

CHAPTER FOUR

My heart was beating furiously in my chest as I stepped through the doorway, with Jay on my heels.

Inside, the room was large, dimly lit, and completely empty. No furniture and no people—except the man who'd opened the door for us. He stood there calmly, watching us with his dark gaze.

The door behind us slid shut.

I surreptitiously wiped my sweaty palms on the front of my dress, hoping the man didn't notice my nervous gesture.

"Hi there," Jay said, stepping up to stand next to me. To my surprise, my friend's voice was steady, and there was a flirtatious smile on his face. "We heard there's a party here. Is that true?"

The man didn't reply for a moment, causing my

anxiety to spike. Then he spoke, his deep voice filled with amusement. "You could say that."

"Great." Jay beamed at him. "That's what we're here for."

I felt a wave of admiration for my friend. I'd always known Jay was great in social situations, but this was far from a typical party setting. For all his reluctance to be here, Jay had clearly brought his A-game.

"Both of you?" the man asked, still sounding amused.

"Yes." I forced a bright smile to my lips. If Jay could do this, so could I. "We're very… curious."

"Ah." The man laughed, a low, sensuous sound that sent a shiver down my spine. "Curious, indeed. Well, follow me."

He turned and began walking toward the far side of the room. My heart skipped a beat. Like the Ks I'd seen on TV, the man didn't just walk; he flowed, his every movement filled with inhuman power and grace.

There was no longer any doubt.

I'd just met my first Krinar.

Jay touched my arm, and my gaze flew up to his. On his face, I could see the same awe and excitement I was feeling. "Oh, my God," I mouthed at him, and he nodded, his eyes wide with shock.

"Come on," I mouthed again, jerking my chin in

the direction of the K, and we both hurried after him, nearly running to keep up.

The K stopped in front of a wall at the far end of the room and waved his hand in a brief motion. To my shock, the wall dissolved, creating an oval, man-sized opening. I barely suppressed a gasp. I'd known that the Ks had more advanced technology, of course, but I'd never seen it in action.

This was definitely going into my article.

As I mentally composed the first paragraph of my story, the K stepped through the opening and disappeared inside. Not wanting to lose him, I stepped through the opening too, with Jay following.

We ended up in a darkened hallway. After walking a dozen feet, we found ourselves in front of another wall. The K waited for us to catch up, and then he created a second opening, through which I could see multi-colored lights and hear pulsing music.

"Here we are," the K said, his English as perfect as any American's. I had always wondered about that—how the aliens knew Earth languages so well. It was speculated that they had some kind of neural language implants, but no one knew for sure.

It might be another thing for me to investigate tonight.

"Wow, how cool," Jay exclaimed, playing his role

of a ditzy party-goer to perfection. "I love the way you do that, man."

The K lifted his eyebrows but didn't dignify that statement with a response. Instead, he went in, walking with that startling, animal-like grace. Jay, who seemed to have gotten over his cautious spell, followed him without hesitation. After a momentary pause, I went after them, my heart pounding with a mixture of trepidation and excitement.

We were officially inside an x-club.

⁓

THE FIRST THING I NOTICED WAS THE MUSIC. OUTSIDE the opening, I'd caught just the pulsing beat, but as soon as I stepped inside, I could hear the weeping undertones of some unknown instrument mixed in with the sharper vibrations. The music wasn't particularly loud, yet it enveloped me, made me feel cocooned within the melody.

Over the music, I could hear laughter and a hum of conversations. The spacious room was filled with people—although I wasn't sure "people" was the right term, given that many of the individuals present were Krinar. The aliens were easy to spot: all of them were tall, dark-haired, and had the kind of stunning beauty one usually observed in supermodels. For a while, there had been rumors that the Ks weren't biological beings at all, and I could see how those rumors had originated. Not only were the Ks incredibly strong and fast, but they were also almost too perfect to be real.

Or at least too perfect to be human.

The room itself was sparsely furnished, with circular tables standing in each corner. They appeared to be the K version of bars. I could see both humans and Ks milling around those tables, holding glasses with various drinks.

The lighting in the room was soft, several hues of warm colors blended together. It flattered the light-colored clothing worn by the Ks. The clothes themselves weren't particularly exotic—pale, floaty dresses for women and shorts with sleeveless shirts for men—but they suited the aliens, emphasizing their golden skin tone and fit, graceful bodies.

Before I could absorb any more details, the K who'd brought us in turned to look at me. There was a mocking half-smile on his full, perfectly shaped lips.

"Curiosity satisfied?" he purred, staring at me, and my breath caught in my throat as I got a good look at him for the first time.

The Krinar standing in front of me had a dark, satyr-like beauty that was both alluring and disturbing. His black hair was glossy and straight, long enough to cover his ears and fall carelessly across his forehead. With his masculine nose and strong jaw, he could've posed for an army-recruitment ad—except no soldier had a mouth so wickedly sensuous or eyes that spoke of such carnal pleasures.

Beautiful, thickly lashed black-brown eyes that were even now traveling over my curves with unabashed male interest.

For the first time in my adult life, I blushed. I couldn't help it. It felt like the K was stripping me with his gaze, leaving me standing there naked and vulnerable. My body felt uncomfortably warm, and my breathing quickened, my pulse speeding up.

The K wasn't just looking at me; he was devouring me with his eyes—and my body was reacting to his stare as if to a physical touch. My nipples hardened, and liquid heat began to gather between my thighs. The air was so thick with sexual tension I could practically taste it. As the K's eyes came up to rest on my face, all I could do was stare at him, hopelessly caught by that dark, all-consuming gaze.

"And who is this, Vair?" A woman's voice broke the spell, intruding into the sensual bubble that seemed to have formed between me and the K.

Grateful for the interruption, I drew in a shuddering breath and tore my eyes away from the Krinar, turning toward the newcomer.

It was another K. The woman was smiling seductively, her attention focused on Jay—who was gaping at her with the same helpless fascination I had just experienced.

Crap. This was not good. This was not good at all. Jay wasn't exactly known for his self-control around temptation—and the female Krinar standing next to him was nothing if not tempting.

Dressed in a short white dress, she was nearly six feet tall, with bronzed, toned legs that seemed to stretch into infinity. Her body was perfectly proportioned, slim and feminine at the same time, with a waist that was almost too small for her frame. "Alien Barbie" was the thought that popped into my head.

A *very sexy* alien Barbie.

"These are a couple of strays I found in the hallway," the K—Vair—responded to the woman's question. His lush lips curved in a sardonic smile as he said, "Shira, meet curious girl and curious boy. Delicious, aren't they?"

Before I could figure out how to react to that insulting—and rather alarming—statement, Jay stepped forward and extended his hand. "I'm Jay," he said in a husky tone. "It's a pleasure to meet you... Shira, is it?"

The woman laughed, her voice low and throaty. "Yes, indeed, sweet thing. It's Shira. Why don't I show you around?" And clasping Jay's proffered hand with her long fingers, she led my friend toward one of the bars, her body moving as sinuously as a cat's.

Jay went with her without a word of protest, apparently too mesmerized to remember his earlier concerns—or the fact that he was here to help me with the story, not to be some K Barbie's sex toy for the night.

"Don't worry," Vair said, as though reading my mind. His voice was filled with dark amusement. "Shira will take care of him."

Reluctantly, I turned toward him, my heartbeat accelerating as our eyes met once again. "I'm not worried," I managed to respond. "We're here to have fun, after all."

"Of course you are, darling." Vair's teeth flashed white. "And fun you shall have. Would you like something to drink, or would you prefer to dance?"

I blinked at him. "Dance?" The music had a good tempo, but it wasn't exactly dance-floor loud. And no one around us was dancing.

Not to mention, I wasn't going within touching distance of Vair if I could help it. The club may have been a place to hook up with Ks, but that wasn't what I was here for.

"Yes, dance." His smile widened at my incredulous look. "Like this." He made a small gesture with his hand, and all of a sudden, the room darkened, the soft light taking on a reddish-purple hue. The music picked up the pace and grew in volume, the throbbing beat permeating my body. All around us, I could feel the energy of the room changing as conversations trailed off and groups coalesced into pairs, beginning to sway in unmistakably dance-like movements.

Startled, I stepped back. "What? How—"

"I own this place," Vair murmured, moving closer to me. "Did I neglect to mention that?"

I swallowed. "Um, yeah. I think you did." *Holy fuck.* This was the club owner—and he seemed to want me for some reason. This was either a big problem or a big opportunity.

"How long have you owned it?" I asked, my inner reporter deciding that it was the latter. This was an excellent chance to get some information—even if it meant I'd have to put up with an alien's sexual advances.

Which weren't nearly as unwelcome as I would've liked.

"A while." Vair stepped even closer, stopping less than a foot away from me.

I sucked in my breath, tilting my head back to gaze up at him. It was like looking up at a mountain. I'd known he was tall, of course, but I hadn't realized how freaking *large* he was. The K was well over six feet in height, with muscles that would've done a bodybuilder proud. He towered over my five-foot-five frame, making me feel as tiny as a child. Even as a human man, he would've been incredibly strong, and the Krinar were known to be much, much stronger than humans.

My belly clenched with fear and arousal as I reflected on the fact that he could do anything he wanted to me. *Anything at all.* Like Jay had said, the Ks were, for all intents and purposes, above the law.

"How long is a while?" I persisted, doing my best to ignore my skyrocketing pulse. "Ever since you guys arrived?"

He laughed. "No. Only since things settled down."

Ah. We were finally getting somewhere. I guessed that "things settling down" was a euphemism for the end of the Great Panic—the dark months that had followed the Ks' arrival on Earth. By that timeline, the club had been around less than eighteen months.

Mentally jotting down that tidbit, I gave Vair an encouraging smile. "How amazing. And what prompted you to open one in New York? I thought that you don't like our cities—"

"Why wouldn't I like your cities?" He quirked his eyebrows.

"Not you personally. I'm talking about your people. The Krinar."

He looked amused. "I can't speak for the Krinar

as a whole, darling, just like you can't speak for the entire population of Earth. I'm just one individual, and I happen to like this city of yours. I find it very... stimulating." His eyes slid down my body again, leaving no doubt about the kind of stimulation he had in mind.

A treacherous warmth kindled in my cheeks as my body reacted to that look again. "Right, of course," I murmured, racking my brain for a way to turn the conversation to a less sexually charged topic. "So why—"

"Why don't we dance?" Vair interrupted, and I realized that nearly everyone around us was swaying and gyrating to the music—including Jay and his Barbie on the other side of the room.

And before I could figure out how to refuse, Vair closed the remaining distance between us, pulling me into his embrace.

CHAPTER FIVE

As Vair's powerful arms closed around me, drawing me against his muscular body, my breathing turned fast and irregular. I could feel his warmth, smell his clean masculine scent, and a wave of heat spread through me, making my inner muscles tighten with need.

Shocked and embarrassed by the potency of my reaction, I attempted to pull away, splaying my palms on Vair's chest to keep him at a distance. "Wait, I'm not good at dancing—"

"You don't need to be." He smiled down at me, ignoring my weak attempts to push him away. "I'll lead."

"But—"

"Just relax, darling," he murmured, beginning to move to the pulsing beat. The steely muscles in his chest flexed under my fingertips, and his thigh brushed against my legs, causing my heartbeat to spike. "Isn't this what you came for?"

I drew in a shaky breath, my mind racing as I stared up at his dark, sensual gaze. *No*, I wanted to scream. *No, it wasn't.*

"I just wanted to see how things were," I whispered instead, hoping the half-truth wouldn't get me kicked out. My voice sounded breathless, as if I'd sprinted a mile. "I'd never seen one of you in person, and I was curious, like I told you…"

"Ah, yes, that infamous curiosity of yours." His smile took on a mocking edge. "You do know what this place is for, don't you, little human?"

I moistened my lower lip, willing my frantic heartbeat to slow. "Of course. But I'd like to just observe this first time. I hope it's not a problem." If it was, I'd have to leave, as I had no intention of sleeping with anyone to get a story.

I wasn't *that* dedicated to my career.

At my response, Vair's eyes darkened, and the smile faded from his lips. "I see."

I waited for him to say something else, but he didn't. Instead, he kept his hold on me, leaving me no choice but to move with him to the music. His hands were gentle on my waist, yet every time I tried to pull away, his grip tightened, making it clear he wasn't quite ready to let me go. After a couple of attempts to discreetly extricate myself from his embrace, I gave up, not wanting to cause a scene.

Just a dance, I told myself. *It's only a dance.* I was fine with a dance if he didn't insist on anything more—and he didn't seem inclined to, for now at least. He held me at a careful distance, close enough for me to be acutely aware of his warm, muscular body, but not so close that I'd be plastered against him. A couple of times, I thought I felt something hard brush against my belly, but I couldn't be sure as the contact was brief.

Still, the idea that it could've been his erection—*that he wanted me like that*—was nearly as exciting as it was scary.

Article. Focus on the article, Amy. "So, Vair, tell me a little bit about yourself." I kept my gaze locked on his face, hoping that talking would distract me from the growing ache in my core. "What made you decide to come to Earth?"

He smiled, his eyes gleaming. "I was bored."

"Bored?" I hadn't expected that. "Why?"

"Because I ran out of ways to amuse myself on Krina. I require a lot of amusement, you see."

I wet my lips again. I had a feeling we were once more venturing into dangerous territory. "What did you do on Krina? Professionally, I mean?" Did the Ks even have jobs? I wasn't sure, but it seemed like a safer topic than whatever it was Vair did to "amuse" himself.

"Professionally?" His smile turned sardonic. "Not much. Or too much. Depends on your perspective, I guess."

"Oh." I stared at him, puzzled. "You mean you changed your career?"

"You could call it that." He laughed softly, looking down at me. "What about you, little human? What is it that you do… professionally?"

"I'm a grad student," I lied. "I'm getting my Master's in English Literature."

"Your Master's?" He lifted his eyebrows.

I felt myself flushing for some reason. "It's an advanced degree one gets after college," I explained, unsure if Vair was messing with me or if he was genuinely unfamiliar with the term. "One step above a Bachelor's degree."

"Ah, okay." His eyes glittered as he shifted his grip on me, his hands moving lower to rest on my hips. "One step above a bachelor. I get it."

He *was* messing with me. "Yes, that's right," I said smoothly, trying to ignore the fact that his large palms were essentially on my ass. "What kind of degrees do you guys have? Do you have college and such?"

He shook his head. "No, we don't. We learn throughout our lives."

"But how do you train for work?" I persisted. "Surely you're not born knowing how to do everything. And what about math, science, history? How do you learn all that?"

"You *are* a curious little creature." He regarded me with a strange half-smile. "You want to know everything about us, don't you?"

"Of course." I gave him a bright smile. "Who wouldn't?"

"Most humans who come here," he murmured, looking at me. "Nearly all of them, in fact. They're interested in only one thing—and that thing has nothing to do with our educational system."

"I guess I'm an exception then," I said, my heart jumping at the odd intensity in his gaze. Was it possible he suspected me for some reason? "I've always loved learning about other cultures—the more exotic, the better."

He laughed softly and stopped, letting me go. Before I could breathe a sigh of relief, I saw that we were standing in front of one of the bars. Somehow Vair had maneuvered us there without my noticing.

"A drink?" he asked, reaching for a glass filled with a purple liquid.

I hesitated. "What is it? Wine?"

"No, just a special type of fruit juice mixed with mild alcohol. It's safe for human consumption."

I considered that for a moment, then accepted

the drink from him, trying not to react when I felt his fingers brush against my own. But I couldn't control a slight hitch in my breathing, and I saw the corners of his lips lift in a knowing smile.

Vair could sense the impact he had on me, and he was obviously enjoying it.

Seeking to hide my discomfort, I lifted the glass to my lips and took a sip. My taste buds exploded at the sweet yet zesty flavor. I could feel the bite of the alcohol, but it was too subtle to detract from the unusual taste of the juice. "What fruit is this made from?" I asked, and Vair grinned at me, sipping his own drink.

"You wouldn't recognize the name if I told you. It's a plant we brought from Krina."

"Oh, wow." I tried the drink again, attempting to memorize the complex flavor so I could describe it in my article later. It made my mouth tingle and my throat feel warm, though that could've been from the alcohol. A part of me wondered if I should've been more careful about trying an exotic drink—or drinking with Vair in general—but I could see other humans in the club holding similar glasses, and it would've been suspicious if I'd refused to so much as take a sip.

Especially given my act as a party girl interested in all things Krinar.

Casting a quick glance around the room, I

spotted Jay dancing on the other side. This time, in addition to the K Barbie—Shira—there was a male Krinar there. The three of them were grinding against each other, and the expression on Jay's face left no doubt that my friend was in seventh heaven, his earlier worries gone.

"Are you involved with him?" Vair stepped in front of me, blocking my line of vision. His tone was casual, but there was an odd expression on his face. "With that pretty boy human?"

I blinked. "With Jay? No."

"Why not?"

"I don't know," I said honestly. "We've just never connected on that level, I guess."

I'd met Jay during our internship at the newspaper, and gotten to know him better when we'd both ended up working there full-time after college. For some reason, Jay—who did his best to have sex with anything that moved—had never tried to hook up with me, and as time passed, I'd found myself soliciting his advice on everything from vacation destinations to boyfriend troubles. In return, I'd lent a sympathetic ear whenever he'd needed to gripe about his overachieving family, and offered him a woman's perspective on clinging one-night stands. Over time, we'd become surprisingly close friends—and all without the attraction that typically accompanied such male-female relationships.

"That's good," Vair murmured, placing his empty glass on a nearby table. "I'm glad to hear that."

I, finishing my own drink, nearly choked on the sweet liquid. There was something almost *possessive* in the way Vair was looking at me. His stare spoke of heated male intent and something more.

Something that disturbed me greatly.

Placing my drink on the bar table, I gave him a cautious smile and took a couple of steps back. "Thank you for the drink and the dance, but I think I have to get going now." My voice sounded steady, even as my heart hammered in my throat. "It's getting late, and I have a lot of work to do tomorrow."

"I thought you were a student." Vair stepped closer, ignoring my obvious desire to maintain a distance between us. "Getting your Master's, isn't that right?"

I swallowed. "Yes, of course. I just meant that I have a lot of work to do on my thesis." *Shit.* He did suspect something—or else he simply enjoyed toying with me, making me nervous. Either way, I needed to get Jay and get out of here.

I was starting to have a bad feeling about all this.

"I don't think your friend is quite ready to leave," Vair said, glancing at Jay—who was happily sandwiched between the Barbie and the male Krinar. "In fact, I'm pretty sure he'd prefer to stay." Vair's voice was filled with amusement, but his eyes gleamed darkly as he turned his attention back to me and said softly, "You should stay as well, darling—learn some more about us."

I opened my mouth to decline his offer, but at that moment, the lights dimmed further and the music changed, becoming twice as loud. I could no longer see my friend on the other side of the room; the dark red glow barely allowed me to discern Vair's features, and he was standing right in front of me.

"Wait—" I began, unnerved by the sudden change of atmosphere, but Vair was already pulling me into his arms again and maneuvering us back into the dancing crowd.

CHAPTER SIX

Startled and alarmed, I pushed at Vair, but it was like trying to move a wall. All I could do was follow his lead as he swayed in a sensuous rhythm, keeping me pressed tightly against him. The music blared all around us, the beat fast and exotic, and his heat, his scent, surrounded me, entangling me in a darkly seductive web. He was so strong my feet barely touched the floor as he held me; it was as though I were a rag doll, an inanimate object he could move about at will.

This time, he didn't bother keeping any distance between us. I could feel every inch of his powerfully muscled body, and I realized with a jolt of panic that he was already hard, his erection pressing into my belly. Gasping, I tried to push at him again, but he ignored my ineffectual struggles, holding me contained without any apparent effort. His eyes glittered in the darkness, watching me with obvious hunger, and my heart thumped harder in my chest as I realized he had no intention of letting me go this time.

Not until he got what he wanted from me.

The thought should've been terrifying, but my body's response had nothing to do with fear. My nipples pebbled within the confines of my bra, and I could feel warm moisture dampening my underwear. My body wanted him with a primitive animal instinct, and it didn't care about the fact that this was happening against my will—that my mind wanted nothing to do with Vair.

As our forced dance continued, the night took on a surreal feel for me. Everything about this place felt like a dream, from the flickering red glow emanating from some invisible light source to the stunningly beautiful man who held me trapped in his embrace. The music pulsed in tune to the throbbing in my body, and my head spun, my senses utterly overwhelmed. The drink, I thought vaguely, staring up at him, but I knew alcohol was only partially responsible for the haze clouding my brain.

It was *him.* Vair was the reason I was feeling like this. My attraction to him was more potent than anything I had ever experienced—and judging by the hard bulge pushing against my stomach, he wanted me just as much. His gaze spoke of dark pleasures and twisted sheets, of ecstasy and lust. My hands moved up to rest on his shoulders as I stopped trying to push him away, and his eyes gleamed brighter at my tacit surrender.

I wasn't sure how much time passed as we danced like that. All of my senses were focused on him—on the hard press of his body against my own and the warm scent of his skin... on the way he held me, with one hand splayed on my upper back and another arm wrapped around my waist. We moved as one, our bodies seemingly in tune, though I didn't have the freedom to move any differently. After a while, his hand slid from my upper back to my neck, his fingers delving under my hair and stroking the bare skin of my nape, and the heat inside me intensified, my breathing coming faster.

When he bent his head and claimed my lips, it was almost a relief, though it added to the tension building inside me, sharpened my need even more. There was no uncertainty in the way he took my mouth, no hesitation of any kind. Vair kissed like he danced—with dominant expertise and calm force, his lips and tongue teasing and invading at the same time. He didn't ask for my response; he demanded it, and I couldn't help but give it to him, my hands clinging to his shoulders and my lips parting to let him in.

My back met a hard surface, and I realized we'd somehow ended up near a wall. Before I could gather my wits, one of his hands slid into my hair, cupping my skull, and his other hand traveled lower, to the curve of my ass. Still kissing me, he lifted me off the ground with one hand, holding me pinned up against the wall so he could grind his erection into the soft notch between my legs. The hard pressure added to the tension in my core, and I moaned into his mouth, unable to control myself.

"Yes, that's it, darling," he whispered, his breath hot on my ear as his mouth trailed over the side of my face. His lips nibbled at my earlobe, and then he bit it lightly, sending goosebumps over that side of my body. "Such a beautiful, delicious little darling…"

I moaned again, my eyes closing and my head arching back as he began kissing the underside of my jaw, his mouth leaving a warm, moist trail on my skin. Rationally, I knew this was wrong, but rationality was not what ruled my mind at the moment. My body was on fire, and my sex pulsed with an empty ache. "Please," I whispered desperately. "Please, Vair…" I didn't know if I was asking him to stop or to continue, and ultimately it didn't matter. I was completely in his power, my body his to play with and manipulate at will.

He chuckled, the sound low and dark, and then his mouth moved lower, to the sensitive curve of my neck. I felt his teeth graze my skin, and the slight pain somehow only added to my arousal, making me writhe against him. "Yes, that's it," he muttered thickly, his hand tightening on my ass. "That's it, darling..."

Lost in my heated need, I barely registered the fact that the wall behind my back seemed to disappear. It was only when I found myself stretched out on some sort of comfortable surface that the warning bells rang in my mind.

Where was I?

Panic swept through me, temporarily clearing away the haze. Gasping, I opened my eyes and saw Vair's bronzed face looming over me. The music still played, the lights still flickered, but we were no longer among the dancing crowd. Instead, we were in some private space, with me laid out flat on a bed-like surface.

"What... where—" I began in shock, and he lowered his head, taking my mouth again. At the same time, he captured my wrists, stretching my arms up over my head before transferring both of my wrists to one of his large hands.

I was now completely helpless, restrained and utterly at his mercy.

The realization should've cooled my desire, but

as soon as he started kissing me again, a melting languor spread through my body, sapping my inclination to fight. Waves of heat rolled over my skin, and my nipples throbbed, becoming acutely sensitive. Warm slickness gathered between my legs, and as Vair ran his free hand down the front of my dress, I unconsciously arched into his touch, desperately craving more.

As my eyes drifted shut, the sense of unreality that had engulfed me earlier returned. It felt like it was all a dream, a dark fantasy playing out only in my mind. When Vair hooked his fingers into the top of my dress and ripped it down the middle, I jerked at the sudden violence of the movement, but even that was not enough to pull me out of my sensual daze. All that existed in my world was heat and pleasure, his touch and the weight of his body over me.

My bra and panties suffered the same fate as my dress, and then he slithered down my body, releasing my wrists to cup my breasts in both of his big hands. His mouth latched onto my nipples, first one, then the other, making me cry out at the sharp, pulling pressure. My hands, finally freed from his restraining hold, somehow found their way to his head, and I clutched fistfuls of his silky hair, not knowing if I was trying to push him away or bring him closer.

He moved up over me then, covering me with his huge, naked body, and I realized that his clothes were gone too, though I didn't remember seeing him remove them. I didn't have a chance to ponder the mystery, though, because everywhere our skin touched, my flesh tingled, as if electrified. Opening my eyes, I met his gaze and saw the same desperate hunger reflected on his face.

He wanted me.

He wanted me, and he was going to take me.

His knees wedged themselves between my legs, spreading them open, and my breath caught as I felt the smooth, broad head of his cock brushing against my inner thigh. Though I couldn't see it, his erection felt massive, and my muscles tensed with a purely feminine fear. Would he hurt me? What if our species weren't as sexually compatible as I'd heard?

It was too late to worry about that, however. Before I could say anything, he kissed me again, claiming my mouth with devastating expertise, and guided himself to my entrance.

His penetration was slow and careful, giving me time to adjust to his girth. Nevertheless, I felt almost painfully stretched as he worked himself in, inch by thick inch. My hands tightened in his hair, and I would've cried out, but he kept his mouth on me, distracting me with delicious, drugging kisses. It wasn't until he was all the way inside me that he let me come up for air, and all I could do at that point was stare at him, panting, my body full and overtaken, completely overwhelmed by his possession.

He stayed still for a moment, holding my gaze, and then he began to move, his strokes leisurely at first and then gradually picking up pace. After a few moments, my discomfort lessened, replaced by steadily growing heat. My eyes closed again, and my hands slid down to his sides, clutching at them as the tension inside me intensified, every thrust sending me spiraling higher and higher. I could hear my own cries and gasping moans, and my knees came up, my legs folding around his hips, bringing him deeper into me. The sensations that rocked my body were so intense I felt as if I would fly apart... and finally, I did, the orgasm rushing through me with unbelievable, shattering force. My body convulsed, my inner muscles contracting around him, and I heard him groan, his cock jerking within me as he reached his own peak.

It's over, I thought dazedly, too stunned to move. Tiny aftershocks of pleasure still rippled through my body, and I felt as if my muscles had turned to jelly. My hands were still grasping at his sides, my nails digging into his skin, and I forced myself to lower my hands to the mattress—or to whatever comfortable surface I was lying on.

Then I slowly opened my eyes and looked at Vair.

He was propped up on his elbows, staring down at me. His breathing was heavier than normal, and his somewhat softer cock was still buried deep inside my body. As our eyes locked, I saw that the heat in his gaze had cooled only slightly—and much to my shock, felt him stiffening within me once again.

"Are you all right?" he asked softly, and I nodded automatically. My body still pulsed from my release, my flesh slick and swollen around his hardening cock, and my mind was in complete turmoil.

I, who had always been so careful and cautious about bed partners, had just had sex with a man I barely knew.

No, not with a man. With a male K—an alien who had invaded my body as unceremoniously as his species had taken over my planet.

"Good," Vair whispered, a dark smile playing on his lips as he began to move inside me again. "Because I'm not done with you yet, little human…"

Mute with shock, I stared up at him, unable to believe this was happening—and that my body was responding again. Even the soreness I was beginning to feel didn't seem to matter; every stroke of his cock was reigniting the fire within me, making me burn with need once again. My hands instinctively rose, gripping his sides once more, and my bent knees tightened around his hips.

"Yes, just like that, darling," he murmured, lowering his head to nuzzle at my neck. His warm lips pressed against the sensitive skin just below my earlobe, and I shivered with pleasure, arching toward him in a silent plea for more. "So sweet, just like I knew you would be…"

As he continued thrusting with a steady rhythm, his mouth teased and nibbled at my neck, and one of his hands worked its way between our bodies, delving into my wet folds. My clit throbbed at his touch, and I tensed as I felt another orgasm approaching. Before I could go over the edge, however, I felt something slice across my neck—a stinging burn that was as painful as it was shocking.

Startled, I cried out, bucking against him as I felt his mouth latch on to the wounded spot. *Those vampirism rumors*, I thought in panic, *they had to be true…* and then I couldn't think at all as my senses exploded in white-hot ecstasy. The climax that had hovered so near swept over me but didn't stop; the sensations intensified instead of ebbing as I screamed out my release. My skin burned, my heart raced, and I was cognizant of nothing but the intense, mind-shattering pleasure. The sucking pull of his mouth at my neck, the driving force of his cock—those were the only things real in my world, and I screamed as my body convulsed over and over again in unrelenting, agonizing bliss.

I wasn't sure how long that went on. It could've been hours or days. All I knew was that the ecstasy seemed to go on forever, until my body and mind couldn't cope with it anymore, and I passed out in Vair's dark embrace.

CHAPTER SEVEN

The alarm buzzed insistently, dragging me out of a sound sleep. Groaning, I rolled over and smacked the annoying clock, desperate to shut it up. The buzzing stopped, and I groaned again, pulling my covers over my head.

Ugh. I really didn't want to go to work. How could it be Monday already? It was just Friday—

Friday! Jackknifing to a sitting position, I gaped at my bedroom walls, my heart beating wildly in my chest as memories of Friday night flooded my brain. I'd gone to an x-club with Jay... I'd danced with a K... I'd had *sex* with that K, and then—

Holy fucking shit. Had Vair bitten me? My hand flew up to my neck, but all I could feel was smooth skin. In general, my body seemed to be free of any pain, though I distinctly remembered feeling sore after the first fucking last night—and if my blurry memory of the second, third, and fourth encounters was in any way accurate, I should've been in serious discomfort. Had I dreamed up the whole thing, and if not, what the hell had happened and how had I ended up in my own apartment?

Jumping out of bed, I ran to the dresser, where my small handbag was sitting. Grabbing it, I fished out my phone and stared at the screen, my breath whooshing out in relief as I saw the date.

It was Saturday. I hadn't lost the entire weekend; I must've simply forgotten to turn off my alarm before I went to bed last night.

Except I didn't remember going to bed last night, I thought with a deep inner chill. The last thing I recalled clearly was that strange, mindless ecstasy after Vair had bitten me—or whatever it was that he'd done to my neck. A cold shudder ran through me at the memory, and it was only then that I realized I was standing there naked.

Completely naked—when I usually slept in a tank top and cotton briefs.

Someone had put me to bed last night... and that someone hadn't been myself.

For the first time, it dawned on me that someone —most likely the K—had been to my apartment.

Maybe was still *in* my apartment.

I nearly hyperventilated at the thought.

"Hello?" I called out, my voice shaking. Frantically opening the dresser, I grabbed the nearest T-shirt and a pair of yoga pants and pulled them on. "Hello? Anyone there?"

Silence was my only response.

Picking up the phone, I opened the bedroom door and crept out into my tiny living room, trying to convince myself not to panic. Maybe it all *had* been a dream, and I'd just had too much to drink with Jay again. Maybe I'd fallen into bed naked and simply didn't remember it. Weird things happened when Jay-style partying was involved.

Jay! My pulse spiked again as I remembered that he had been there with me—and that when I'd seen him last, he'd been gearing up for a close encounter with not one but two Krinar. What happened to him? Where was he now?

To my tremendous relief, the living room was empty—as were the kitchen and the bathroom. My apartment was tiny, just a converted studio, so there weren't many places a K could hide. I was alone and safe for now.

Still shaking from the surge of adrenaline, I sat down at the kitchen table and dialed Jay's number. He didn't pick up right away, and just when I thought I would go out of my mind with panic, I heard his sleep-roughened voice answer, "Hello?"

"Jay!" I almost broke into tears. "Jay, are you okay?"

"What? Oh... Amy?" He sounded disoriented. "What—what's going on?"

"Jay, what happened last night?"

"Last night?" I could practically hear the wheels starting to turn in his sleep-fogged brain. "Last night... Oh shit, baby girl, we went to the club! The fucking x-club! Are you okay? You disappeared with that K and then—"

"What happened to *you*?" I interrupted, not wanting to talk about my experience quite yet. "Did you sleep with those two Ks?"

Jay laughed with delight. "Sleep with them? Baby girl, we did everything *but* sleep, and it was the most intense shit I'd ever experienced—like Ecstasy combined with heroin and amplified tenfold. I don't even know how I ended up home. We must've been partying all night 'cause I don't remember a thing right now."

"Right, uh-huh." I rubbed the bridge of my nose, the adrenaline draining out of me. It sounded like Jay had gone through the same experience that I had. Whatever had happened to us last night was far outside the realm of normal sex, corroborating all those stories I'd read online.

I was certain now that the night had been real—

which left the mystery of how I'd ended up back home after passing out at the club.

Or at least I assumed I'd passed out at the club, as my last memories were of non-stop sex and impossibly intense pleasure.

As Jay continued to talk, telling me all about how the K Barbie had gone down on him while she was being fucked by the male Krinar, I tried to work through the possibilities. The only thing that made any sense was that Vair had brought me home... which meant he knew who I was and where I lived.

He must've found my driver's license in my purse, I decided after a moment of uneasy contemplation. If he knew more than that about me—if he knew I was a journalist—I doubted he would've let me go so easily.

I got lucky, and so did Jay.

When he finished describing his sexcapade, I told him about what had happened to me, leaving out the forceful nature of Vair's seduction and my own helpless reaction to it. The fact that I'd ended up having sex against my better judgment—and that it had been the hottest sex of my life—was not something I wanted to analyze too closely.

"Wow, you go, baby girl," Jay said admiringly when I was done telling him the night's events in broad strokes. "You really let loose this time. I'm proud of you. So what's next? Are you going to go back to the club?"

"No," I said. One night of out-of-this-world sex was plenty for me. "Next, I write the story."

It was time for my real career to begin.

Part Two

VAIR

CHAPTER EIGHT

The memory of his hands gripping and positioning my hips encroached upon my mind as my fingertips clacked noisily against the keyboard. The words on the screen in front of me blurred, and I yet again lost focus on the article I was writing as I recalled the way he'd slowly rocked his impossible girth into me from behind, how his tongue had licked between my shoulder blades and his teeth had teased my earlobe, his fingers circling maddeningly, teasing my drenched clit until I'd—

Fuck.

It had been happening all day. One minute, I would be on my virtual soapbox espousing the benefits of eating bone broth and bacon, citing Paleo diet research and case studies, and the next, I'd be in a near frenzy—skin flushed, thighs rhythmically clenching beneath my desk as I remembered the inconceivably rapturous sensation of having him inside me.

God, it had been like nothing I'd ever felt before.

Or would again.

Because I'd fucked an alien.

It was a hard fact that played on a loop inside my head throughout the day.

Every day.

All day.

In the morning as I ate my breakfast, while I sat in meetings at work, when I rode the subway, as I was washing my hair in the shower—*particularly while in the shower.* Even in sleep I would dream about him.

It had been a month. Four weeks, two days, and thirteen hours since I'd ventured into an alien sex club in the Meatpacking District of New York City.

The gravity of what I'd done that night confounded me daily still, but it was the magnitude of the situation I had since trapped myself in that was becoming more suffocating by the hour.

I couldn't forget about it for a moment, and the knowledge that my present predicament was entirely my fault didn't help.

Because the truth was, I could've walked away. Twice. Before I'd slept with the gorgeous x-club owner, and then afterward.

I could've locked that absolutely mind-blowing experience away, never letting a soul other than my coworker and partner in alien-sex-clubbing, Jay, know about anything that had happened.

But instead, I did what any ambitious twenty-four-year-old with a mountain of student loan debt would've done.

I'd penned an alien sex tell-all article for *The New York Herald*.

Only… I hadn't exactly told *all*. I'd done what good journalists are supposed to do. I'd removed myself personally from all events revealed in my alien sexposé and reported that it was based off of my interviews with *other* undisclosed humans.

And I'd gotten away with it. *So far*. Which was what confused and concerned me most, feeding my paranoia and driving my fear of imminent alien retaliation to new heights with each passing day.

My computer pinged, and a small email alert popped up in the lower right-hand corner of my left screen. Noting the sender, I clicked the "x" button at the corner of the pop-up to dismiss it. I had a deadline to meet and couldn't afford to be by ridiculous emails from my mom tonight—any more distracted than I already was, that is.

Another ping sounded, followed by another pop-up alert. I sighed and waited it out as eight more pings and pop-ups appeared. She was on a roll for a

Friday night. After the eleventh pop-up, I went to my browser and logged out of my personal Outlook account.

My mother had been a "sky is falling" Chicken Little type long before the Krinar had actually fallen from the sky two years ago to take control of Earth. Her initial "told you so" victory dance amid the early invasion panic had been quickly followed by daily email forwards from random online "news" sources predicting all of the horrible ways humans were bound to be mistreated and ultimately killed by the Ks.

My mother's propensity for readily embracing irrational and absurd media sources *might* have played a small role in influencing my desire to seek and report the facts above all else in my career as a journalist.

Unfortunately, facts were often slanted by other factors. And truth came in shades beyond black and white.

As "accurate" as my alien sexposé had been, it hadn't exactly been impartial.

Not only had my acclaimed article omitted all culpability on my part as a willing participant in the best sexual experience of my life, but it had also painted the Ks in a rather negative light, showcasing them as sexual predators whose blood-drawing had an Ecstasy-like, aphrodisiac effect upon humans.

In quieter moments, I could admit that perhaps that specific slant was driven by my own ego's need to rationalize my embarrassing response to Vair that night.

Throughout my college years, I'd always been so careful, so cautious about the few men I'd dated. I'd become friends with all of my boyfriends first, getting to know them well before things had become sexual. I'd never even come close to having a one-night stand.

And then, a month ago, the very first time I'd let loose and allowed passion to dictate my actions, I'd gone and had a one-night stand with a deadly, vampiric extraterrestrial who'd sucked my blood and fucked me until I'd literally collapsed unconscious from sexual exhaustion.

My phone buzzed to life on my desk, startling me. My mother's number lit up the screen.

Oh, what the hell. Not like I was getting work done anyway. Talking to my mom would be the fastest, surest way to get my errant mind off sex.

I hit the speaker button. "Hey, Ma."

"Did you read my email?"

"You mean the *dozen* emails you sent me ten seconds ago?"

"Yeah." She said this with zero hesitation or apology.

I bit the smile forming on my lips and shook my

head at the ceiling. "Nope. Still at work. Got an article deadline."

There was a sharp intake of breath from the other end of the line, followed by a clattering noise and then muffled shouting for my dad to come quickly.

"You're not still working there, are you?" She sounded out of breath now. "I thought you decided last week you were going to quit *The Herald* and go into hiding?"

"No. *You* decided I should quit and go into hiding." I lowered the speaker volume. I was pretty sure I was the only one still working on my side of the floor, but just in case.

"You're not writing another E.T. article, I hope?"

"Yep. That's sort of my thing now, Ma. I get all the Krinar stories."

Another sharp inhale, followed by a wheezing sound. "Have more victimized xenophiles come forward with their sex-clubbing stories?"

I winced. Xenophiles—or xenos for short—was the derogatory term for humans who lusted after Ks and sought out sexual relations with them. "K addicts" was another, more neutral name for them. It was that disturbing phenomenon that had spawned the xeno clubs—a.k.a. x-clubs—that I'd reported on in my article.

"No." I cleared my throat. "This one's about their

forced vegan lifestyle and how it's not only robbing humans of our free will but potentially damaging our health and the health of future generations, simply for the sake of satisfying *their* preferences."

Two years ago, when the Krinar species had invaded and assumed control of Earth, they'd inserted themselves into all aspects of our world—down to the foods readily available for consumption. They had immediately shut down our industrial farming industry and forced meat and dairy producers to grow fruits and vegetables instead. Nowadays, any meat or dairy products to be found were sold at an outrageous premium.

The Ks claimed to have done this for our own benefit, to prevent us from further destroying our already weakened, sickly bodies and our even sicklier planet with our overproduction and overconsumption of meat and dairy.

And this had pretty well set the tone for how we could expect to be viewed by our new overlords—as a lower life form not intelligent enough to make even the most basic daily choices about the foods we put into our bodies.

"But you've been a vegan for eight years." My dad's voice sounded confused.

"Oh, hey, Dad. Yeah, that's true. But that's not the point. The point is, it's our right to—"

"The point is, why should *we* have to give up pork

fat when they're eating humans at dance clubs," my mother cut in with exasperation.

Oh, Jesus. "Listen, I've got to get back to work. I'll call you guys on Sunday, all right?"

"Amy." My dad's voice was calm but weighted with concern. "We think you need to stop antagonizing the Ks with these articles. From what little we know of them, they're a violent, dangerous species… capable of anything. It isn't wise to risk—"

"You have to stop!" My mother's frantic pitch was approaching E-flat range. "Your dad and I are worried sick that those E.T.s are going to come to kill you and eat your brain any minute now."

I knew I shouldn't have picked up her call. "It's blood they like, Ma. Not brains."

"They eat brains too," she insisted. "I sent you a YouTube interview on it."

Here we go. "Okay, remember when we discussed YouTube not being the most reliable—"

"The YouTube video of those Saudi resistors being massacred by Ks was confirmed to be legit," my dad reminded me. "No one thought that footage could possibly be real at first either."

He had a point, although I wouldn't concede to it just now. "That was different, Dad."

The memory of that early video footage of the Ks never failed to induce an internal shudder. During the first few weeks of the Krinar invasion, guerrilla fighters in the Middle East had ambushed a small group of unarmed Ks. The gruesome event that ensued had been captured via iPhone, showing the whole world exactly what kind of genetically advanced—and positively ruthless—species had taken over planet Earth. Thirty-some Saudis armed with grenades and automatic assault weapons had been no match for six unarmed Ks capable of moving at inhuman speed and strong enough to literally tear their human attackers apart with bare hands—and throw them as far as sixty feet with minimal effort.

"Sources say they're constructing human labor camps in Costa Rica," my dad continued.

I sighed and let my eyes roll. *"Sources"* indeed.

"They're developing torture and execution facilities for miscreant humans," my mother interjected.

This was too much. I needed to get back to work.

"Your mother read that they publicly behead criminals on their home planet of Krina."

"And then they have a feast where they drink their blood and eat their brains and other organs," she chimed in.

Ugh. My empty stomach churned in revolt. "Guys, I really have to go now; my boss just emailed me for an update."

"All right, honey, but your mother and I are very

worried. We respect what you're trying to do for the good of the public, but we think it'd be better if you went into hiding and wrote for one of the underground news sources we subscribe to."

Of course they did. "Thanks, Dad. But you don't have to worry about me. Everything's fine. Believe me, if the Ks had been upset over my x-club story, they would've pulled it from circulation as soon as it was released. They never would've let it get so much press and media attention." At least I hoped so. *I had been banking on that theory.* "It's not like *The New York Herald* is beyond their reach or influence. It's been pretty well confirmed that Ks monitor and control the world media at this point."

"You say that now, but what happens when they come after you and cart you off to a K torture camp"—my mom's voice cracked on an exaggerated, hysterical sob—"and we're left wondering how many aliens ate our little girl's brains for supper?"

With a poorly muffled wail of distress, she sobbed out a melodramatic goodbye and audibly stomped off.

That was my mother. If there was one thing she could always be counted on for, it was her penchant for high doomsday drama and her knack for saying the most unhelpful, inappropriate, and terrifying things at inopportune moments.

A long, awkward pause on the line followed.

Twenty-seven years of marriage and my dad had never quite learned how to react to my mom's special brand of crazy. It was an odd thing between the two of them that had grated on me immensely growing up.

Eventually, he said, "I should probably let you go now."

"'Kay, Dad. Call you on Sunday."

"Talk to you then. Be careful, Amy."

CHAPTER NINE

I DISCONNECTED THE CALL AND RESUMED TYPING, pushing my parents' dysfunctional relationship and my mom's crazy K fears far from my mind as I quoted research from the Weston A. Price Foundation extolling the merits of lard, full-fat butter, and cod liver oil consumption.

The Krinar were a highly intelligent, ancient species that clearly held a genetic advantage over humans, given what we had witnessed as far as their physical capabilities, not to mention what we had been told of their extended life spans. They'd taken over Earth in a matter of weeks, wielding technology more impressive than anything our science fiction novels had ever contemplated. And although we were similar in appearance to them—albeit far less beautiful and perfect-looking—by the

Krinar's own admission, our human DNA was actually more similar to that of a gorilla than that of a Krinar.

Therefore, who the hell were they to decide what *we* should eat?

I chose to ignore the fact that gorillas were herbivores—because it was irrelevant to my point. *Sort of.*

And besides, if a vegan diet was so fulfilling to them as a species, why did they crave our blood so much? Maybe it was *they* who were missing something from this perfect vegan diet of theirs that they'd now subjected our entire planet to. And what if the same missing link in their diet led to humans eventually craving blood as well?

Fuck. I removed my glasses and rubbed my eyes. I was going off the rails and reasoning like my mother now.

My mind drifted to thoughts of Vair—specifically, the way he'd bitten me that night at the club—and I wondered what my blood had tasted like to him. Just thinking about the way his bite had *felt* always got me uncomfortably aroused. It was a memory I'd pleasured myself to on more than one occasion—more often than I cared to contemplate.

What if I was becoming a xeno?

The notion terrified me—and turned me on.

I couldn't stop thinking about him.

Too often I'd lie awake at night, wondering what he was doing at that very moment. I'd even go so far as to run through alternate scenarios in my head about how things might play out if I ever got the courage to get out of bed, get dressed, and go back to his club.

Proof-positive I was going insane.

In some scenarios, I imagined him being terribly angry with me for the article I'd written about his club—possibly reacting with violence. That potential alone was enough to keep me from ever venturing back. Other times, I envisioned him mocking me for coming back, laughing in my face and tossing me out of the club.

Yet somehow I felt it was more likely he'd forgotten about me altogether by now—too busy sucking and fucking New York City's finest supermodels, no doubt.

Ironically, rather than ruin business for Vair, the article I'd written had made his x-club the most sought-after secret sex club in Manhattan. Instead of being warned away, humans were more curious than ever to explore the sexual proclivities of the Ks, resulting in more eager xenos than before.

I shook my head. I'd inadvertently done Vair a favor with my article. He had no reason to be mad.

But beyond that, I doubted he'd be too terribly concerned with me one way or another, based on the fact that I *had* heard from Vair—just once—right after my story was printed.

An enormous exotic fruit basket had been delivered to me at *The Herald*. And by exotic, I mean the basket was filled with fruits that couldn't have been grown anywhere on Earth. I'd been terrified to even touch it, but Jay had dug right in, rummaging through and examining each unusual, delicious-looking piece of edible perfection.

There'd been a note with the basket. And the few words written in bold, black scrawl on the rectangular-shaped, cream-colored cardstock had nearly sent me into cardiac arrest.

Delicious thesis, darling. Cheers to earning your Master's!

I'd reread those words only a few thousand times, making myself—as well as Jay—a nervous wreck by analyzing every possible overt and hidden message contained therein, only to resign myself to the fact that Vair was once again messing with me, teasing me and fucking with my head like the inferior human specimen that he clearly took me for.

No wonder he'd seemed so amused when I'd lied about being a grad student earning my Master's.

I decided his note was Vair-speak equivalent for: *"Congratulations. I was on to you all along from the moment you entered my club, and I played you right back."*

Because he *had* played me.

I'd succumbed all too easily to his undeniable sexual thrall.

And he was letting me know that he didn't give a fuck about my little article, while making it painfully clear that he still held all the power—and that he could use it to crush me if he chose to.

He knew where I lived. Where I worked. He knew the truth of what had happened between us. He was above the law—as were all Ks—and far higher up on the food chain than I was.

But he let the article run and my white lie stand because he simply didn't care one way or another.

That conclusion alone should've been a relief to me.

But it wasn't. For some reason, it infuriated me to my very core.

Against Jay's protests, I'd pitched that giant, fancy exotic fruit basket straight down the incinerator chute along with Vair's mocking card that same evening.

And I'd committed myself to writing any and every anti-K story that *The Herald* would print going forward.

∽

My fingers were flying over the keyboard when

both of the computer screens in front of me flickered, then went dark.

My palm connected with the wood laminate desktop as I silently cursed *The Herald's* quest to cut costs and their ever-cheapening technology systems.

I glanced at my watch. It was after seven p.m.

Great. No one in IT would be around.

Leaning forward, I reached behind the monitors to fiddle with the connection, hoping it was just a loose cable, when my screens abruptly came back on, along with my speakers—at max volume.

I froze, my heart seizing in my chest at the sights and sounds that assaulted me.

The right monitor displayed footage of me from my night at the x-club—my writhing body held high in Vair's arms, dress hiked up to my waist, back pressed against the wall. My lust-dazed face was plainly visible, my plaintive cry of "Please, Vair" distinctly audible over the pulsing background beat of club music as the gorgeous alien ground himself rhythmically between my spread thighs.

The incriminating scenes playing out on the left monitor were far worse, the sounds more embarrassing still. I stopped breathing as a high-def montage of our tangled, glistening naked bodies copulating in every manner and position imaginable streamed across my screen.

I was *so* fucked.

CHAPTER TEN

"Cab!" I yelled at the security guys in the lobby downstairs over the file boxes balanced precariously in my arms. "Please," I appended when out of the corner of my eye, I saw one of the guards literally jump and scramble for the phone next to him at the front desk.

In my effort to keep my voice from cracking, I'd managed to sound like a royal bitch.

The other guard rushed forward to help me with my boxes, and I lost my composure again, barking, "I got it!"

I was too close to an epic meltdown for any sort of interaction, and the file boxes packed to the gills with my personal belongings were a physical barrier I wasn't willing to part with at the moment. They were heavy and awkward, but I needed some sort of energy outlet for the adrenaline coursing through me.

"I'll wait outside," I announced, cutting the first security guard off as he started to say that a cab was on its way.

Utilizing what my ex-boyfriend had often said was my strongest asset, I hip-checked the swinging glass exit door wide—with more force than was probably necessary—before guard number two had a chance to get it for me.

"Thanks," I muttered in a belated effort at politeness as I plowed through, rear first.

The scents of early fall in New York City filled my lungs as I backed my stack of haphazardly packed belongings out onto the sidewalk on wobbly limbs.

"Hey! Watch where you're going!" a woman snapped at me when I spun around without looking and nearly rammed into her with my awkward burden.

"Sorry."

Jesus, I needed to pull it together. I had to figure out what to do next, where I could go for help.

Could anyone even help me?

How bad was my situation? How many news stations and social media outlets had already received that footage?

Would my mother see it?

My dad?

My eyes burned with unshed tears, and my stomach lurched. *Great.* I was about to vomit all over Broadway.

Where was that cab?

I forced in a calming breath as a cool evening breeze whipped my hair. Peering around the side of my boxes as best I could to avoid colliding with another pedestrian, I inched closer to the curb. Twilight was waning, and while the street was active, I was grateful that there were far more popular spots than Lower Manhattan's Financial District for the masses to seek early entertainment on a Friday night.

Tires rolled to a stop a few feet from the curb in front of me, and I craned my neck enough to make out a black stretch limo—not the cab I'd been hoping for. I started to amble on farther down the sidewalk to where a cabbie would be better able to spot me, when I heard the sound of car doors opening.

Sure, rapid footsteps fell smoothly upon the concrete in my direction.

Too smoothly.

Some innate self-preservation instinct made my pulse quicken. I had a mad compulsion to drop my boxes and flee, but I was wearing my practical two-inch heels paired with a very impractical pencil skirt. It was doubtful I'd be able to outrun a K.

A second later, it was too late entirely as I sensed *his* heat at my back—running along the entire length of my body, blocking out any trace of the evening breeze. I froze as the familiar scent of inhuman male perfection assaulted my olfaction, bringing with it the memory of the most carnally gratifying night of my life.

Oh, fuck.

My stomach clenched. My nipples hardened. The rest of my body seemed to have a vivid memory of that night as well, judging by its immediate—and mortifying—Pavlovian response to Vair's mere presence. My inner muscles fluttered in anticipation, slick heat rushing to lubricate my sex.

I reminded my stupid sex that this was the same alien who had just destroyed my career and my life. He was the enemy who had invaded my planet. *An enemy who was possibly about to kill me as well.*

Or worse—turn me over to Krinar authorities.

But when warm, long fingers encircled my right bicep, another jolt of sexual electricity shot through me. And when his other hand latched onto my left hip, it felt oddly reassuring, momentarily calming and centering me as a second set of unseen hands pulled the file boxes from my grasp.

"This way, darling," Vair's deep voice instructed from above my head as he bodily steered me in the direction of the stretch limo.

To the person who had confiscated my file boxes, Vair spoke rapidly in a foreign, guttural-sounding language that I couldn't place. Over my shoulder, I glimpsed a tall, beautiful male K in a black suit nodding in assent as he effortlessly hauled my boxes back in the direction of the building where I worked.

Had worked. Wait…

"That's my stuff," I protested a little too late. "Where's he going? Why's he taking my stuff?"

"Get in the car, Amy." The command was accompanied by gentle pressure at my crown as Vair physically maneuvered me into the limousine before I had sense enough to put up a fight.

He followed closely behind, folding his huge form gracefully into the luxuriously upholstered passenger cab and taking the seat across from me. The car began moving while I remained stock still—frozen in place amid a mixture of heart-pounding shock, fear, and anticipation.

The moment Vair was settled and his full attention was fixed upon me where we sat face to face, I blushed. And not just a little flush that could pass for nervousness or be attributed to recent exertion from the heavy boxes I'd carried, either. It was the kind that made my skin feel sun-blistered and my head dizzy. The kind that screamed "guilty" in a court of law.

The sort of blush that broadcast exactly how well

I remembered the sensation of him plunging deep inside me and the sound of his masculine groans and grunts as he spent himself in me… in my mouth… across my back, my stomach, my…

I broke eye contact—for fear of passing out—and let my eyes roam about as if investigating my surroundings. But I barely took in any of it. Every cell and fiber of my being was too acutely aware of the god-like alien sitting across from me.

Watching me.

God, he was so much better-looking than my masturbatory sessions had given him credit for. So much bigger. More predatory.

Way more dangerous.

There was too much room in his enormous limo for just the two of us. Yet not nearly enough space for me to avoid the sight, the scent, the very vibration of his essence in the air surrounding me.

He could be taking me anywhere. Planning to do any number of terrible things to me.

Pull it together, Amy.

"You look hot." His deep voice was light and playful, but it startled me just the same. "Shall I adjust the temperature?"

My eyes snapped back to him and found that he was staring down at his palm—tracing something there with the forefinger of his other hand and not looking at me at all. He was wearing casual slacks, a simple white T-shirt that accentuated his bronzed skin tone, and loafers, and he managed to look fresh and chic—more sophisticated than I'd looked first thing this morning in my pencil skirt and silk blouse... *before* I was rumpled and disheveled from my day.

"What are you going to do to me?" My voice betrayed me, emerging too high-pitched and with a slight quiver. Pitiable-sounding. *Damn it.*

He seemed taken aback by my question at first—or perhaps by my tone—as he returned his attention to me, but then a slow, sensuous smile spread across his wide mouth and full lips. "What indeed?" His forefinger brushed absently across those gorgeous lips, and I had to remind myself to focus on his mocking tone—and on finding a way to live through this.

"What would you do if you were in my shoes?" He sighed, and his face was suddenly devoid of humor. "I'm afraid several very powerful Krinar Council members were rather displeased with your article."

There it was. My very worst fear realized. I was a dead woman.

And it was bullshit. My mother could *not* be right about this.

"What?" I feigned shock. "What do you mean?" I blustered, a surge of adrenaline fueling me. "I was simply presenting factual information about your club... about the sexual habits of your race. I mean... you can't be serious? You're not serious, are you?" I latched onto the offensive and ran with it. "My God, your club is now the most sought-after best-kept secret in town. I've got New York's hottest supermodels calling me, begging for your address!"

I'd failed to mask the jealousy in my voice at that last part, so I quickly rambled on. "And anyway, I was under the impression that your powerful Council members controlled our media. I thought they'd simply squash the article—erase it from online circulation entirely—if they didn't like what I'd written."

Vair's features remained impassive. Uncompromising.

Fuck.

Fear and panic had my mouth working overtime. "They *let* it run," I emphasized, as if that alone signified their tacit endorsement of it. "Well, I'm sorry; I had no idea anyone would be offended." I threw in a huff of confusion. "If they disapproved, why didn't they just pull it? It can't be my fault they failed to pull it? I mean, they could've just called *The Herald* and asked them to pu—"

I stopped at the sound of Vair's slow clapping and the look of mocking amusement in his dark eyes.

"Thank you for that lovely, very insincere

apology, Ms. Myers. A pity you didn't take up acting while you were at NYU earning your degree in journalism."

Shit. I really was in trouble.

He held my gaze in silence, and the air around me seemed to grow colder with each passing second.

"So… what then?" I raised one haughty, exasperated brow and emitted a dry chuckle that came out sounding far too nervous to support my bluff. "You going to cart me off to K jail? Or is capital punishment customary for alien-sexing-n-telling?" *Oh my God, shut up!*

"Mmm… a bit of torture, a decade in a Krinar hard labor camp, and then public beheading. *Customarily.*"

This couldn't be happening. My mother's wacky sources could not be accurate. There was no way. He was messing with me. I was sure of it.

Almost.

I released a nervous laugh. His expression remained stoic.

"Y-you're not serious…"

He frowned and ran a hand through his tousled hair. Now he looked pissed. "I convinced them it would be bad PR to torture and kill you."

"Oh?" My monosyllabic response somehow managed to affect effortless nonchalance—while my heart began to pump overtime.

Was he fucking with me or was he serious? I'd lost the ability to gauge.

"The Council agreed that I would be allowed to… handle the situation with you. Directly." His eyes had darkened at "handle," sending an involuntary shiver through me.

"W-what does that mean?" That he personally got to torture and kill me? *Somewhere away from prying human eyes?* Was that where we were headed now?

My face must've projected my train of thought because he rolled his eyes in a surprisingly human-like manner, then muttered something in that guttural foreign language he'd used before. Probably Krinar cuss words, judging from the angry set of his jaw and the way his big hands had balled into fists against the seat on either side of him.

But when he addressed me again, his voice was gentle. Patient. "We don't practice capital punishment on Krina. Our methods for reforming those who break our laws are very different from what you're accustomed to in human society. No Krinar will harm you. Least of all me."

His eyes on me were thoughtful as he said it. Forthright. They didn't look like they wanted to hurt me at all. Those bottomless eyes looked like they wanted something else entirely. And in my haze of relief, I suddenly wanted to drown in them—to cast years of sanity and sound judgment aside and believe anything they said.

I blinked and looked away, breaking the connection as I recalled the grainy YouTube footage of those Saudis being torn apart.

"Ks *have* killed humans," I pointed out. *Because facts were facts*—no matter what voodoo his eyes made me feel. "It's been documented. Graphically," I added with a grimace of disgust.

"Yes, it's true," he acknowledged. "We have killed humans when necessary. Mostly in self-defense as a last resort."

It was my turn to roll my eyes. But I chose not to debate it further, my mind shifting to my initial cause for panic this evening.

The video footage.

If they didn't intend to harm me physically in retaliation for my article, then there was another reason for this meeting. And for that footage.

My pulse raced as it hit me. *They were blackmailing me?*

Horror and excitement gripped me at once. If I was right and they intended to blackmail me with it, then there was a chance the video hadn't been released to the masses yet. And I would do anything to prevent its release. Even if it meant…

Fine. It was inevitable.

"You want me to retract what I wrote in my article," I stated, my voice flat. My career as a journalist would be over, but at least I'd walk away with some shred of dignity if I could keep that sex tape out of circulation.

He frowned. "Of course not. Your exposé was brilliant. And"—his tongue ran casually across his full bottom lip as his gaze swept over me—"enlightening."

The heat that pooled anew in my belly was as untimely as it was unwelcome.

I gave myself a mental shake. "You don't want me to retract what I said?" A sense of dread crept up my spine at the realization that I might not have any bargaining chip at all.

"No." His lips parted in a lazy smile as his dark eyes held mine.

Then his gaze fell to my breasts.

My palms were slick with sweat where they gripped the leather seat beneath me. I swallowed. Breathed. "Why the video footage then?"

He leaned forward, his expression deathly serious as reproving eyes returned to mine. "You didn't call, Amy."

It was as if all the air had suddenly been sucked out of the limo.

"You never came back to my club."

I'd soaked through my panties by "Amy"—in spite

of the confusion and mild terror that his abruptly accusatory tone evoked.

"I didn't know you wanted me to." The truth tumbled out defensively, faster than I could process what he'd said as conflicting emotions flared to life within me. "I mean—I didn't mean for anything to happen… with you… that night at the club."

What the hell was I saying?

What was he saying?

A bead of sweat trickled down between my shoulder blades, causing me to shiver in my silk blouse. It was freezing in the limo now.

"I see. You were a victim then?" His tone was earnest, but his eyes appeared amused. Smug.

I felt my anger rising. There was no easy answer to his question. I kept my knees glued together and my sweaty palms planted on the seat in an effort to subvert my shaking.

"I never meant for anything to happen between us that night," I reiterated, my words clear and firm despite the dryness now choking my throat.

He sighed. "Humans complicate the most basic emotions by experiencing them through extraneous social filters." His eyes projected a strange sort of pity—and a measure of quiet disappointment that was somehow unsettling.

I needed water. *I needed out of Vair's limo.*

I needed answers more.

"Is it on the internet already?" I blurted, my heart pounding in my ears.

"Is what on the internet, love?"

"You know what!"

"Answer my question, and I'll answer yours," he countered.

"I'm not a victim."

"Good." He gave a curt nod and proceeded to retrieve a glass bottle of clear liquid from a refrigerated side compartment. "I don't play well with victims."

He uncapped the bottle and held it out to me.

"I'm not drinking that."

"It's water, Amy."

"And what else?"

He smirked and shook his head, murmuring, "Whatever else you want, darling." He proceeded to give me a lazy, blatant once-over reminiscent of the flirtatious, teasing manner he'd taken with me during our initial meeting at his club.

His all-consuming gaze held the promise of so much more than water. And it had the same spellbinding effect as before, drawing me in and making me want things I rationally shouldn't, leaving me feeling confused, vulnerable, and exposed.

He shifted his big body forward to the edge of his seat, grazing my bare knee with the cold bottle in the process, and I jerked back reflexively.

With a chuckle, he tipped the bottle up to his own mouth, and I found myself riveted by the sight of his lips pressed against the bottle's opening, of his throat muscles working as he gulped down half the contents of the glass container.

When he'd drunk his fill, he offered it to me again with a raised brow, and I didn't hesitate to wrench it from his grasp. I rationalized it was because I was parched, and not because I was answering his unspoken challenge—or because I had some mad impulse to put my mouth where his had been.

It was a safe bet it wasn't poisoned. A powerful alien didn't need poisoned water to get whatever it was he wanted from me. I just needed to figure out what that something was, if it wasn't the retraction of my x-club story that he was after.

Brazenly wrapping my lips around the bottle's opening, I tipped my head back and chugged the remains of the container in one noisy, unladylike pull. *Because fuck the Ks with their constant superiority bullshit and their ongoing intimidation of my race.*

My thirst quenched and a sliver of my dignity returning, I lowered the bottle along with my chin, releasing an uncouth, open-mouthed sigh of satisfaction in the process. Only to have my stomach fall straight through the floor at the look on Vair's face.

It was the look of a jungle cat ready to pounce. The face of a starving man intent on his favorite meal.

I cleared my throat. Gripping the empty glass bottle with both hands, I held it primly in front of me—suspended above my lap, as if it might shield me from him.

"The internet," I prompted. "I answered your question. Now answer mine."

"No."

My stomach twisted at his brusque reply. "No? You won't answer?"

"No, it's not on the internet," he clarified, his face suddenly a stone mask, his tone formal. Irritated. "Yet."

I swallowed. "I see. So"—I rolled and squeezed the glass bottle between clammy fingers—"is it on its way to being released to the media then?"

"No."

My immediate sense of relief was fleeting as I summoned the courage to push forward and ask, "So what do you want from me? In exchange for keeping it off the internet?"

He laughed. It was a throaty, dark chuckle that sent goosebumps flowering over my skin. He waved his hand, and a three-dimensional video image appeared out of thin air directly between us. A perfectly detailed, lifelike hologram proceeded to play, as if from an unseen projector.

A hologram of me.

"Let's discuss this video first, shall we?"

It was footage of me in my office from not more than thirty minutes ago. Multiple camera angles had captured every embarrassing moment, from my stunned reaction to the sex montage when it had first appeared on my desktop screens, to the freak-out that had ensued as I'd attempted to shut the videos off to no avail—first by disconnecting the monitors, then disconnecting my computer, then yanking every cord from the wall outlet, until finally I'd succumbed to full meltdown panic and resorted to smashing both monitors to pieces with the closest thing to a weapon that I'd been able to get my hands on: my Swingline twenty-sheet, three-prong hole puncher.

Not my finest moment under pressure.

CHAPTER ELEVEN

I wasn't sure what was more disturbing: seeing myself flip out and destroy the newspaper's property in a fit of panic, or knowing that Vair—and perhaps other Ks—had been invading my privacy and spying on me.

Definitely the latter, I decided—although the former was more mortifying in the moment.

I was speechless as I watched the hologram version of myself calm down enough to realize what I'd done and allow a new sense of horror to take hold.

"Imagine how it hurt my feelings," Vair's smooth voice cut in as the hologram "me" proceeded to dash about, packing up my personal belongings as quickly as possible, "to see this—your violent reaction to my favorite compilation of our intimate moments together?"

He was messing with me again.

Or he was a psycho.

Leave it to me to have my first one-night stand with a *Fatal Attraction* vampire alien.

It should've been a tip-off when he'd told me on the dance floor that he'd come to Earth out of boredom. He'd said he required a lot of amusement, and that he had run out of ways to amuse himself on Krina. *So he'd left his home planet to open a sex club in NYC centered around Ks sucking and fucking willing humans?*

And I'd viewed my ex-boyfriend's lack of direction in life as a red flag of things to come.

"You threw out the exotic fruit basket I sent you." His voice held a note of censure.

Vair just *had* to be messing with me. I tried to tune him out and focus on the hologram version of myself shoving papers and mementos into emptied file boxes. My hologram was out of breath.

I was out of breath. I shut my eyes as my head began to spin.

"Amy?"

I shook my head, unwilling to open my eyes. I didn't want to see him.

But then I heard him. *Grunting.*

Followed by the sound of a woman moaning.

And I knew without looking that it was another hologram version of me that was playing now. Of us. From our night at the club.

"Oh, please, Vair. Right there... yesss..."

The sound of slick flesh slapping together filled the limo at high volume, along with the sound of my own whimpered pleas and cries for more.

Oh, God.

The bottle slipped from my fingers.

"Amy?" Present-moment Vair's calm entreaty was overlaid by the sounds of my unseen hologram self reaching orgasm.

I couldn't breathe. I pressed my fingers to my temples.

"You're so wet," his hypnotic voice spoke from across the limo.

My inner muscles contracted, clenching around emptiness.

"So ready for me."

Fuck. *I was very wet.*

I could feel his eyes on me, sense his essence calling to me—his sexual hunger a visceral thing that pulsed and tugged at my core as his need became my need, magnifying it tenfold.

"I've thought about you." His voice was low and hoarse. "Did you think about me?"

I'd thought about him nearly every moment of every day for the past month.

"Take your clothes off."

I shook my head at his directive, even as I reached for the buttons of my blouse and began to undo them with trembling fingers.

"That's it... Such a beautiful, delicious little human," he purred at me over the background sounds of my hologram's moaning and soft sucking noises.

Recorded Vair was grunting louder now, and my sex throbbed in reply, aching with an intensifying need at his growled commands for me to suck him harder. *Deeper.*

My mouth watered. My fingers fumbled desperately, tugging at the stubborn buttons.

This was madness.

"Amy," Vair called quietly to me again.

I opened my eyes at last.

The lighting had changed. The limo's tinted windows had darkened to black, and a soft, flickering red glow similar to the lighting in his x-club illuminated the alien predator seated across from me.

Naked.

Stroking the biggest erection I'd ever seen.

And between us, the projected 3D recordings of our naked bodies were 69-ing like starved animals.

"Come here." One hand fisted the base of his

massive cock while he crooked the finger of his other hand at me. "Show me you're not a victim."

The strange sense of unreality I'd experienced in his club came over me again, and I found myself on my knees between his muscled thighs a moment later, stretching my lips around the thick, wet tip and sucking him into my mouth—*because attacking his cock with my tongue was apparently the way my brain and body instinctively chose to demonstrate non-victimhood.*

"Ahh—good girl," he hissed, raising his hips toward my mouth while pressing down on the back of my head, quickly filling me to the back of my throat, yet still barely fitting half of his thick length inside.

He pushed deeper. I gagged. He eased back, then shoved forward to the same point again. "That's it, darling…"

My eyes watered as he took up a steady, insistent rhythm, rocking his hips up while restricting the position and motion of my head with his hand, fucking my mouth without ceremony or pretense. Driving into me as far as my gag reflex would allow while his other hand squeezed and stroked the length of him that I was unable to take.

"Yes… just like that," his gruff voice coaxed as crude slurping noises began to escape me—the sounds becoming beyond my ability to control as he pumped faster, taking my mouth with a primal urgency that *was* oddly empowering.

His sharp, short intakes of breath and guttural grunts of satisfaction had me aroused to the point of near orgasm as I was swept up in the paradox of feeling so powerfully in control of delivering his most critical, basic need, while at the same time being dominated by the situation.

"Amy... *Amy...*" He groaned my name like a dirty prayer as his thrusts became erratic.

I was sure he was about to come.

I was on the brink of flying apart myself; even without any physical stimulation, it was all so fucking hot.

His blunt fingertips spread and dragged back and forth across the back of my scalp, sending delightful shivers through me before he fisted the roots of my hair in a near-painful caveman grip.

Knowing he was about to blow in my mouth at any moment, I succumbed to temptation, slipping my hand between my thighs and up my pencil skirt —desperately seeking my own fulfillment.

The moment I pressed my fingertips to my soaked cotton underwear, I came undone.

I'd been hoping to get myself off discreetly while he was caught up in his release—ideally, without him even knowing it. But as soon as I began to detonate, he tugged me sharply up by my hair, pulling himself from my mouth and wrenching my head upright.

My eyes opened wide as my body twisted and convulsed, the carnal sounds erupting from me rivaling those from the recorded hologram playing in the background.

Caught red-handed, with my fingers up my skirt and rubbing in a frantic motion, my flushed face sloppy wet with drool and residual tears from gagging on his cock, I was helpless to halt the sheer force of my own orgasm as he absorbed every brutally raw detail.

I couldn't have pulled my fingers away from my slit if I'd wanted to.

I didn't want to.

The sly, slight smile on his lips was the only thing darker than his eyes as he watched me bare my wanton soul, his jaw tight and his fist locked in a death grip around the base of his massively engorged erection, preventing his own explosion.

CHAPTER TWELVE

"May I?" He swiped his thumb across my bottom lip, wiping the dampness from my chin as his fingers massaged the part of my scalp where he'd pulled my hair.

I wasn't sure how long we'd faced one another in silence in his darkened limo. He'd squeezed the base of his cock until the pained look in his eyes had finally subsided and he was able to release it—still fully erect and loaded—while I had yet to rein in my breathing and get my emotions under control.

The video hologram no longer played. And the limo had stopped moving several minutes ago. But I couldn't bring myself to ask where we were.

I remained mute with shock, still kneeling on the carpeted limo floor between his legs, as he proceeded to pull my hand from between my thighs.

He brought my fingers up to his mouth and licked them clean with a satisfied hum. He then tugged my skirt back down into place and buttoned up my blouse, studying my features closely as he did this—as if I were a puzzle he was working out.

"Are you all right?"

I didn't answer him, too baffled by his seemingly solicitous gestures. Using the pads of his thumbs, he dabbed the dampness from my cheeks just below the rim of my glasses where my eyes had leaked.

What the hell had just happened?

He hadn't even come. He was still sporting monster wood that had to be causing him discomfort. Like *major* discomfort.

Nevertheless, he was calm and in control as his fingertips brushed aside the strands of loose, fine hair that had fallen across my forehead. The last time we'd been together, he'd been insatiable, unable to stop himself from taking me over and over… and over again.

Was he not into me anymore?

His forefinger traced a line between my brows, drawing my attention to the fact I was frowning.

"It's all right, you know," he said gently. "Your responses are perfectly healthy and normal." His smile was kind—genuine and surprisingly open—as he brushed the backs of his knuckles down my jawline. "I like it when you're honest with yourself. I like that light that comes on in your eyes when you see something you want." He bent closer and pressed a small kiss to my cheek. His breath warmed my ear as he murmured, "But what I love most of all is watching you take it."

What?

"Next time"—his voice dropped an octave—"I hope you go for the intimacy you truly crave… that you climb onto my lap and take what you want from me."

Want from him?

Intimacy?

He had me all wrong. I didn't want *anything* from him, least of all intimacy.

I drew my face away, shaking my head minutely as I pulled my shit together about five minutes too late. "That's not… This wasn't—"

"Wait, don't tell me…" His lips quirked as he raised a silencing forefinger. "You never meant for any of this to happen just now, did you?" Mocking Vair was back. "You were simply curious? You only wanted to *observe* this first time, right?" He threw my own words back at me—the excuses I'd given him at the club.

I rolled my eyes away, muttering *"Sonofabitch"* under my breath.

His hand snaked out and fisted the back of my hair with jarring speed, forcing my eyes back to his.

He leaned closer. No longer smiling, he looked like the dark predator he was. He canted his head at me.

I swallowed. *Gulped.*

His long, dark lashes lowered as those deep-set brown eyes dropped to my throat. His gaze settled upon the wild pulse point that had to be visible in my neck, given how frantically I could feel it beating.

He licked his lips. And stared.

And stared.

My breath came in rapid, shallow pants despite my effort to remain calm. Because the more I tried to calm myself, the harder I could feel my heart racing.

His nostrils flared. His face inched ever closer, then dipped to my neck until the tip of his nose grazed my jugular.

He was going to bite me.

Butterflies thrilled in my belly. I braced myself for impact. But he simply inhaled deeply and exhaled. "Delicious."

He released my hair and abruptly pulled away, while I fought yet again to get my breathing under control.

"I'd like for you to come to my club tomorrow night. My driver will pick you up at eleven."

He'd phrased the first part as a request, the

second as a directive. Was he giving me a choice or not?

"What if I don't want to come to your club?"

He leaned back against the plush leather seat cushions, linked his fingers behind his head, and shrugged—utterly unconcerned with the fact that his giant erection stood straight and proud in my direct line of sight. "What if I get lonely and my nostalgia drives me to play home videos of us in Times Square?"

Ass. "What do you want from me?"

"I've just told you, love. I want you to come back to my club."

"For what purpose?"

Another shrug. "I need you there."

My throat felt suddenly tight. I was exhausted and emotionally wrecked from all of Vair's mind games.

"Why?"

He smirked. "Plenty of reasons."

He was planning to humiliate me publicly. It was the obvious conclusion. I bit the inside of my cheek to keep myself from getting emotional. Stoically, I asked, "Is there an option B?"

His perfect, straight white teeth practically glowed in the darkness as he shook his head and chuckled. "No. But I'll hear your suggestion if you have one."

"I'll retract everything I said in my article," I immediately offered.

"No."

"What if I amended it to paint Ks in a more favorable light?"

"No."

"Fine, I'll issue a public apology to all Ks and xenophiles!" I all but screamed at him.

I couldn't go back to his club. I couldn't spend any more time with this man—*alien.*

"No."

"Why not?"

"None of those things are of any interest to me."

"Then what is of interest?"

The electronic limo door swung up, revealing the front entrance of my apartment building. The sight of it was a blessed relief. And at the same time, it was somehow unnerving that this was where he'd taken me.

We were done?

"You're a smart, curious girl, Amy. I'm sure you'll figure it out."

Just like that? He wipes my drool, then kicks me to the curb while calmly sitting back and driving off with a ginormous erection?

Whatever. I scrambled to the door and climbed out with as much dignity as possible, praying that none of my neighbors would be around to see me —*or the monster alien wood dismissing me.*

Thankfully, no one seemed to be around. I swung my head back around to deliver a scathing parting remark, but the limo door was already closing in my face.

Apparently the Krinar weren't big on goodbyes.

I turned and took a step in the direction of my building, only to find the gorgeous male K who had taken my file boxes blocking my path. He held my small purse and my keys out to me.

Oh. Right. Those had been tossed into one of the file boxes he'd confiscated.

"Um. Thank you." I took them from him.

He smiled. His unnaturally perfect face was a vision of symmetry. "You're welcome. Your computer screens have been restored and your office items returned to their usual places," he informed me.

Then he walked off, leaving me standing on the sidewalk more confused than ever.

CHAPTER THIRTEEN

"Intimacy! Can you believe it? He said I craved intimacy. Intimacy from *him*, of all absurd things. As if, right?"

Jay's eyes were the size of saucers. "Could we back up to the part where Vair said several powerful Krinar Council members were upset about your article? Did he assign a number to several? Or did he just say several?"

"Just several." I frowned at the empty wine glass in my hand from my seat on the couch as Jay nervously refilled his own at the kitchen island. "Did you hear what I said about the intimacy part?"

Jay nodded absently and took a liberal sip of red wine.

After Vair had dropped me off, I'd stayed in my own apartment only long enough to pack an overnight bag and to obsess over the many places where Ks could've hidden cameras. Then I'd hightailed it over to Jay's Soho micro-loft. The unit his parents had bought for him was in a swanky building with twenty-four-hour doormen. And while logically, I knew no one was safe from a K, rich people places always *felt* safer somehow.

"I have a friend from college who wound up at the CIA... I think," Jay mused aloud, pacing the small space of his living room with a full wine glass in his unsteady hand. "Maybe he can help us?"

"Um"—I waved my empty glass in the air—"you mind?"

"You can't go back to his club tomorrow night."

"Duh!"

"He could be planning anything."

"Agreed."

"You'd be walking into a trap."

"No shit."

"He could do anything to you in that club and no one would stop him."

"Jay, my insufficient buzz is already wearing off. This conversation isn't helping." I tilted my glass in indication once more.

"We've got to get you out of town tonight, baby girl." He grabbed the wine bottle from the kitchen island and came toward me. "Tomorrow morning at the latest."

"It's not that simple," I said as he refilled my crystal stemware. "I can't risk that video footage being released."

"But it doesn't add up." Jay shook his head. "Why wouldn't he just let you retract what you said or issue a public apology? How does you going to his club appease angry Council members more than a retraction would?"

I managed a shrug as I tipped my wine back.

"It doesn't," Jay concluded, his brow furrowed in concentration as he sank down onto the coffee table in front of me. "You know what I think? I think he knew we were reporters the moment we arrived at his club."

"I've thought that, too. He did personally let us in and escort us inside. How many club owners do that?"

"Exactly. And then he was all over you the whole time. I mean the guy never left your side for even a minute. If I hadn't been so distracted by Shira—fuck, do you suppose he meant for Shira to distract me?"

It had never occurred to me, but Jay was right. He and I had been more or less separated immediately upon entering Vair's club. The alien Barbie had captured Jay's attention and swept him away from my side within moments of Vair introducing her to us.

A strange, disconcerting realization seemed to

cross Jay's features as he slowly eyed me up and down. It looked out of place on his characteristically jovial, pretty-boy face.

"What?" I glanced down to check that I hadn't spilled red wine on myself or on his cream-colored couch. "Why are you looking at me like that?"

He chewed his lip, his frown deepening.

"You're freaking me out, Jay."

"I'm remembering an exchange between Shira and Kyrel," he answered slowly, as if he was still processing the memory. "You know, the male K she and I hooked up with?"

I smiled as a welcome giggle bubbled up in my chest, alleviating some of the tension in the air. "Oh, I remember. You've over-shared quite a few memorable stories about him as well as Shira."

Jay didn't laugh. Or even crack a smile as he scanned me up and down again, as if he were seeing a problem. "Fuck. You really *are* hot, Amy. You know that, right?" He said this like it was bad news.

"Um... yeah? I'm okay-looking, sure. Thanks. So? What did Shira and Kyrel say?"

"When I was dancing between Kyrel and Shira, and I first realized you'd left the dance floor with Vair and were nowhere to be seen, I panicked. I tried to break away, saying I had to find you. Shira stopped me, telling me not to worry, that Vair would take great care of you. Then Kyrel laughed and said,

'Yes, for all eternity, in fact.' I didn't think much of it at the time, assuming it was just—I don't know, the alien expression equivalent of Kubrick's 'me love you long time' joke or something."

I released a breath as my stomach settled in relief. "*That's* what you're freaking me out over?"

"No, it was the part that came after that. Shira laughed along with him, and then she said something about how Ks could be exceptionally possessive. She joked that I was lucky I hadn't been holding your hand in the hallway outside the club, or else I might be dead or minus a hand at the very least."

"What?" My sense of relief was short-lived. "She actually said that? And you took it as a joke—coming from a female alien who literally *could* tear your hand off?" My eyes flew to the ceiling in disbelief. "And you still hooked up with her."

"Look, give me a break. I'm pretty sure her hand was already on my junk at that point. Anyway, who am I to judge an extraterrestrial's quirky sense of humor? Besides, she was a fucking goddess. Hottest woman I've ever seen up close."

"Krinar," I corrected him. "Hottest Krinar."

"Whatever. She was all woman, believe me. And she was warning me about Vair's possessive tendencies, not her own. Because Kyrel cautioned me a moment later that I should be careful never to lay a hand on you if I wanted to go on living. He said"—Jay's brow rose meaningfully, as if this were the key part—"that he'd had to calm Vair down by pointing out that our body language quite obviously said we weren't together when Vair first spotted us waiting in the hallway."

Vair had questioned me directly about my relationship with Jay that night. In truth, it *had* felt strangely possessive at the time—given the fact we'd only just met. But clearly, he'd merely wanted to hook up with me and hadn't wanted any obstacles in his path.

"So... Krinar males are competitive and susceptible to male ego and pride, same as human men? Got it. I'll make that the topic of my next K article."

Jay let out a huff. "Don't you see? Vair saw us before he let us in. As did Kyrel, apparently. So they must've been viewing us on surveillance cameras as we were waiting that long-ass time in the entry hallway."

I recalled how Jay and I had stood there, staring nervously at the big metallic gray door for what had felt like an eternity. I'd had to work up the courage to knock several times before Vair had finally answered and opened the door for us.

I didn't get what Jay thought was so revealing in all of this, though. It was hardly unusual to screen visitors via hidden surveillance at an exclusive Manhattan club, let alone a K sex club.

He groaned at my nonplussed expression, setting the wine bottle down next to him with a heavy thud. "Amy, what if Vair staked his claim on you before we even entered his x-club? What if this blackmail thing has more to do with him wanting you than it does the Krinar Council being upset over your article or wanting to exact some sort of punishment for it?"

My stomach flipped with a level of schoolgirl excitement that was disturbing and altogether embarrassing, given the absurdity of Jay's theory, not to mention the sheer sordidness its entire premise was built upon.

It wasn't as if I actually wanted Vair to want me.

No, what I was feeling was simply the natural relief that anyone would draw from the notion of someone wanting them versus the scarier and yet more likely notion of someone planning to ship them off to a Costa Rican alien labor camp. Because from a purely logical standpoint, this made the terrifying prospect of having to go to Vair's club tomorrow night seem a bit safer—albeit more nerve-racking at the same time.

I shook my head. "I really don't think that's the case, Jay."

"Why not? Hell, he's already caught on to your intimacy issues."

My jaw dropped and I whacked him squarely in the shoulder, coming dangerously close to sloshing my wine all over us both in the process. "Take that back!"

"Annnd"—Jay laughed at my attack, wielding a triumphant forefinger—"he didn't come in your mouth tonight. Baby girl, that alien has got it bad for you."

"Oh, my God, shut up!" I'd known I'd regret telling Jay too many details from my limo encounter with Vair. But I'd been in a vulnerable state and had needed to vent to someone. "That is the most absurd logic ever."

To redirect the conversation away from aborted blowjobs and my perceived intimacy issues, I asked, "Why didn't you tell me about what Shira and Kyrel said?"

"Don't know. Guess I just didn't think of it after everything else that happened that night. It was already a lot to talk about. Like being bitten by a K." He wagged his brows. "That shit was like the best drug ever. Besides, nothing ever came of it. We both made it home safely from the club, and aside from the fruit basket after your article came out, you hadn't heard from Vair until today."

I nodded. It was all too much to contemplate. I felt my body crashing, the adrenaline that had fueled me all evening rapidly waning. Yet my mind remained keyed up. No doubt I'd enjoy a special state of exhaustion combined with insomnia tonight.

"Look, it's just a theory. Don't panic, okay? We'll figure something out."

I closed my eyes, pulled my glasses off, and pinched the bridge of my nose. "Got any Advil? Tylenol?"

"I'll do you one better. Hang on." I heard Jay rise and cross in the direction of the bathroom.

I chuckled dryly to myself, betting he'd be back with some proprietary blend of pharmaceutical-grade marijuana oil.

Blindly, I set my glasses down on the coffee table in front of me. Those things had been bothering me for weeks. I likely needed a new prescription. My vision somehow seemed to be worse whenever I wore them lately, and it was causing me headaches.

What if Vair actually did want me?

Though why would he? For what? He had NYC supermodels and actresses clamoring for his attention.

Besides, it wasn't as if our species were compatible. At least, I didn't think we were. Not really. I pushed aside the memory of how "compatible" we'd felt sexually. It was irrelevant. A farce.

He'd bitten me. That was what had caused the aphrodisiac high I'd experienced with him.

"You look flushed." Jay's voice pulled me from my thoughts as he reentered the room. "I'll get you some water."

He returned with a glass of water and offered me a Xanax pill.

"Jay, I can't take that."

"It's the best thing for my headaches."

"Yeah, 'cause you're passed out."

"It'll help with your anxiety. Amy, we've got less than twenty-four hours to come up with a plan. You can't go back to Vair's club tomorrow night."

"But I've had wine."

"So have I, and I'm taking one. It's the lowest dose. My doctor says it's fine with a little alcohol."

I was about to ask whether that advice was from the same doctor who prescribed his medicinal marijuana, but instead, I gave in and downed the little white pill before I lost my nerve. It was doubtful I'd get any sleep tonight otherwise, and I needed all the mental sharpness I could muster tomorrow to devise a way out of going to Vair's club.

"Take my bed," Jay offered. "I'll take the couch."

"No way. I'll sleep on the couch." Lord only knew who and what had happened in Jay's bed this week and whether his cleaning lady had washed the sheets since.

I was already feeling woozy and swaying on my

feet as I brushed my teeth and washed up in Jay's bathroom.

I'd just managed to pull my pajamas on and climb atop the couch Jay had made up for me when I succumbed to the state of blissful, dreamless darkness that only pharma-induced sleep provides.

CHAPTER FOURTEEN

I awoke to a light shining directly in my eyes as someone pried the lids open. I grumble-moaned my displeasure.

"Relax," Vair's voice soothed in my ear. "Let us have a look, darling." I felt his arms around me. They felt so good, so comforting as they held my dead weight upright in his lap.

I was dreaming. And I didn't want to interrupt what I already sensed was going to be a pleasant dream about Vair.

Even in my dream state, I felt drugged—unnaturally exhausted—making it easier to do as he'd asked and relax into his embrace despite the blinding light presently in my eyes. I reveled in the masculine scent of him, in the sensation of his full lips pressing against my temple and his warm fingers gently stroking the side of my head.

My eyelids were released and the light extinguished. It occurred to me that someone other than Vair had been holding them open. He was talking in that foreign language of his again. And not to me, I deduced when a female voice responded in kind.

Cool, feminine fingers palpated the glands on either side of my neck next, and an irrational sense of jealousy washed over me when Vair laughed softly at whatever the woman who spoke his language had said.

"No," I murmured. "Not funny." I wasn't sure why. And my words came out slurred. Garbled.

They both laughed this time.

"Agreed," Vair said. "It's not at all funny how you make me worry. Never mind the way you disregard your liver."

He was chastising me. But any sense of indignation I might've felt was forgotten as he hugged me tighter against the warm, solid mass of his chest.

Because in that moment, he felt safe. Normal. Better than normal. *Nearly human.*

And in my dream, I believed him. I believed Vair truly was concerned with my well-being. And it felt… nice. So nice that I didn't object when a glass was pressed to my lips and Vair told me to drink.

I swallowed all of the strange-tasting, sweet liquid as he stroked my hair and made promises that I was safe with him, that he would never do anything to harm me.

After a while, I got the sense that we were alone. I didn't open my eyes, though. I was too afraid that the dream would vanish and I'd wake up.

My brain felt more lucid after the drink he'd given me, my tongue certainly more adroit as I mumbled in response that I would never harm him either, and assured him that he was also safe with me… *if* he turned over all copies of that video footage he was blackmailing me with.

My declaration was met with a barely suppressed shout of laughter. I felt his body quake beneath me.

"Clever, delicious little minx," he half-chuckled, half-growled against my neck.

My equilibrium shifted and I found myself flat on my back, trapped beneath him. His weight settled between my legs.

My nipples instantly tightened.

I moaned as his lips brushed mine, his tongue flicking out to tease me as the hard length of his erection did the same, grinding into the soft, pulsating notch between my thighs.

In my dream, I lacked the arm muscle strength

and coordination to reach up and pull his head down to me. But I wanted him to kiss me. *Really* kiss me.

So badly.

Who was I kidding? I wanted him to fuck me. *Consume me.*

I told him so.

He groaned and told me to "shut the fuck up." It sounded so out of calm, collected alien character for him that I giggled. And then he shut me up with his hard, insistent mouth.

The sensation of his tongue thrusting between my lips to stroke my own was torture, especially coupled with the masculine grunts of arousal that reverberated to the back of my throat as he ground his massive cock where I wanted him most.

Torture of the best kind.

"I *should* fuck you," he managed between kisses. He sounded angry.

I liked it.

My inner muscles squeezed in anticipation. My pajama bottoms were already soaked.

"Until you can't"—he thrust his pelvis against me just right—"fucking walk."

"Who's stopping you?" I gasped out.

He growled and rotated his pelvis hard into me once more.

Then twice. And by the third time—

Oh, God...

I was on the brink of orgasm when he stopped, released my mouth, and abruptly pulled his delicious weight from me.

My hands that had been too weak to lift a moment ago were somehow gripping his T-shirt in an effort to halt his retreat. I made a wounded sound that didn't even sound human as his panted breaths fanned my forehead.

"Don't want you to go." My voice emerged shaky. I sounded so forlorn. Lost. So... *needy.*

So god-awful!

I opened my eyes to end this dream-turned-sudden-nightmare and found Vair's hungry gaze studying me through the darkness surrounding us—a pained, vulnerable expression on his face that somehow mirrored my own tortured emotions.

I couldn't decide if I should take comfort in that or feel worse about it.

His irises were so black they were nearly the same shade as his pupils, making him look scary. *And yet hot.*

Creepy otherworldly.

Still hot.

But most of all, he looked real. Very real. Felt real. Smelled real.

"I'm dreaming." *Please say yes. Please say yes.* "This is a dream."

He simply stared. Didn't answer. Eventually, he told me to close my eyes.

I did.

His lips brushed my forehead. He told me he had to leave so I could finish dreaming—neither confirming nor negating whether I was, in fact, dreaming at present.

I was still clutching his T-shirt. He told me to let go, joking that even aliens needed rest on occasion.

"I promise you, I don't want to leave you. But you need your rest now."

He told me he hoped I was brave enough to come to his club that evening. *Way to throw down the gauntlet.* His implication that I had a choice in the matter was as odd as my feelings and behavior toward him in that moment, further corroborating that I *had* to be dreaming.

I felt him gently removing my fingers from his shoulders.

He told me he would stay until I fell asleep. I told him I *was* asleep.

The last thing I remembered was letting him know that he was wrong.

I didn't have an intimacy problem.

CHAPTER FIFTEEN

Someone was singing "Bad Romance." That someone was also cooking eggs and bacon. And hash browns. More importantly, I smelled coffee.

I smiled and rubbed my eyes open. Jay was preparing breakfast less than fifteen feet away in his open kitchen, using animal products that only wealthy people like his parents had easy access to.

"You're an angel," I called out to him, stretching as I rose from my makeshift bed. I felt surprisingly well-rested and energized, my mind clearer than it should've been, my head and body suffering none of the aches and pains I would've expected after consuming wine and Xanax and sleeping on a couch. Even my looming anxiety over the prospect of going to Vair's club tonight had somehow abated during the night, because I felt markedly less panicked over the whole situation.

"So I've been told. Breakfast is in five." He waved a spatula at me. "Chop-chop."

I hit the bathroom, washed up, and was back in ten to take a seat next to Jay at his island countertop. He had already shaved, showered, and dressed for the day—which was atypical Jay behavior for nine a.m. on a Saturday.

"The hash browns, fruit, and coffee are all vegan," he announced proudly, making me laugh as he bit into his bacon.

"Look who's a funny man this morning," I teased, picking up my fork and digging into the hash browns Jay had plated for me.

He seemed to be in remarkable spirits, full of energy and beaming from ear to ear like he couldn't wait to get going with his day. Or to tell me something?

"Did you go out partying after I went to bed last night?"

"Without you?" he exclaimed with a look of mock horror. "I slept great is all. You?"

"Surprisingly excellent as well. Thanks again for letting me stay with you. And for making breakfast."

"My pleasure. Can't let my only female friend face Ks on an empty stomach." He glanced at his watch. "But hurry it up; we've got less than fourteen hours to figure out what you're going to wear tonight to the club, not to mention come up with brilliant interview questions."

I frowned. "I'm sorry, did I miss something? Last night we were plotting my escape from the city. Now you want me to go to Vair's club?"

"I know, I know, but I feel better about the whole situation after sleeping on it. Because guess who's going to the x-club with you?" He raised his brow and gestured to himself.

My eyes popped. "Jay, I can't ask you to do that."

"You're not. I'm crashing your party." He grinned. "I took it upon myself to contact Vair this morning to let him know I'd be coming. Also, to negotiate our terms."

My fork slipped to the quartz countertop with a clatter. "You what?"

"Told him you were only going if I came with you and if he guaranteed our safety." His puppy-brown eyes lit with excitement. *"And* if you got to interview some Ks."

"You spoke with him?"

"No, we texted."

"Texted?" My jaw dropped. "You have Vair's phone number?"

He shrugged, looking sheepish. "I swiped it from your exotic fruit basket."

"What?" There had been no number written on

the card included with the basket Vair had sent me. I'd read that note over a thousand times. "Jay, there was no number anywhere on his card."

"Not on the personal card, no. But there was a business card tucked inside the basket that included a phone number."

"And you kept it all this time and never told me?"

He held his palm up. "You wanted nothing to do with that basket, Amy. You were spazzing out and didn't even want to touch it, remember? I barely had time to look through the cool fruit and snag the card for safekeeping before you tossed the whole thing into the incinerator."

"So you just woke up this morning and texted a K?" I couldn't process it. "You texted Vair?"

He nodded, his mouth now full from the bite of eggs and bacon he'd taken.

"And he responded?"

Another nod. He raised his finger as he finished chewing. "Yeah. He said I could come tonight." He paused to take a sip of coffee. "I asked about the Council members, too. He said everything was cool and he was handling it."

"He said everything was *cool*?"

"I'm paraphrasing. He said you aren't in any danger from them or any other Ks offended by your article as long as you stick close to him. You know, so that he can look out for you. That's why he wants you to come to his club."

Jay said this like it made perfect, rational sense. As if Vair was blackmailing me into coming to his alien sex club for altruistic reasons.

I couldn't decide if I should be relieved and embrace my best friend's abrupt change of perspective on my situation, or be alarmed that I might be living the Krinar version of *Invasion of the Body Snatchers*.

"Come on, eat up. Everything's going to be fine." Jay gave me a reassuring smile. "Think about it: this will be way better material for your next K article than the veganism stuff."

I shook my head, my appetite gone. "What deal did you make with Vair about me interviewing Ks?"

"Like I said, I told Vair you'd come to his club tonight if I came with you, and if you got to interview some Ks who frequent the club for your next article."

"This is a bad idea, Jay." Writing articles about Ks is how I'd gotten myself into this whole mess.

"Will you stop shaking your head at me and listen for a minute? Vair gave me his word that we'd be safe under his protection at the club." He spoke slowly and clearly, as if he thought I wasn't getting it. *As if Vair's word on this was somehow gospel.*

"He also agreed to let you interview Ks, but only

Ks of his choosing." Jay scrunched his nose at the last part—like it was the most regrettable news. "And only on his terms, which include him being present for any and all interviews with these other Ks. For your protection, of course."

Once again, Jay was quick to present Vair's actions as considerate—practically noble. What the heck was going on?

"To be honest, I got the impression Vair just wants you to interview him, actually."

Great. "Jay, you know I want to help get factual information about the Ks out to the public more than anyone, but don't you think I should avoid pissing off the Krinar Council any more than I already have at this point? What if Vair's lying and this is all a trap?"

Jay cocked his head, studying me with a distracted expression.

"If you come with me, we're both endangering our lives," I pointed out. "We could disappear off the face of the Earth, and no one would ever know what happened to us."

Jay's eyes widened, like he'd just had an epiphany. "Hey, you're not wearing your glasses. And you're not squinting at everything like you normally do without them."

"Did you hear anything I just said?"

"I heard it. Are you wearing contacts? I thought

you'd lost your last pair weeks ago and hadn't reordered them yet?"

I was about to flip out on him over his bizarre behavior when I realized he was right; I wasn't wearing my glasses. I *had* lost my contacts weeks ago. Over four weeks ago, to be exact—the night I'd hooked up with Vair.

And I could see fine without glasses or contacts right now. *Perfectly*, in fact.

I could see flecks of gold and black in Jay's brown irises that I'd never noticed before. I could read the tiny print on the dial settings on the small Viking convection oven nestled within the wall of cabinets that was well over six feet behind Jay's back.

"Oh, my God…"

I hopped off my stool and dashed over to the couch. I found my glasses right where I'd left them on the coffee table the night before and put them on.

Then I took them off. And put them back on again.

I couldn't see for shit with them on.

It wasn't a new prescription that I needed. Apparently, I didn't need glasses at all? Something wasn't right.

Then it hit me. *His scent* hit me.

My heart thudded in my chest. I dropped to my ass on the couch, balled the mess of tangled sheets between my hands, and raised them to my face, inhaling deeply as I recalled my dream.

"Um… what are you doing?"

I looked up at Jay. "I think Vair was here."

"Don't be silly. We have doormen downstairs."

"Like that matters. Jay, we watched him disintegrate a wall right in front of us at his club, remember?"

"Point taken." He joined me on the couch. "But maybe it's just my cologne you're smelling." He attempted to pull the sheets from my grasp, and I jerked back reflexively, clutching them to my chest.

Like a possessive, K-sniffing xenophile. A crazed K addict.

I tossed the sheets at Jay like they were on fire.

Subtle.

"No—I mean, it's not, um… your scent." I took my glasses off and busied my fingers by fiddling with the hinges. "You can sniff for yourself." I sounded like a lunatic.

The look on my best friend's face confirmed my worst fear. I put my glasses back on.

Perfect vision was overrated.

He stood. "Okay. Ah, suppose it's from your limo ride yesterday then? You didn't shower last night, right?"

It was a perfectly plausible explanation. But somehow I knew my gut was right this time. Vair had been here. And I had very confusing mixed feelings about that.

My body did too.

"You're probably right."

"Of course I'm right. I'm always right," Jay said with a forced laugh, doing his best to lighten the mood. "But why don't I try to connect with that friend of mine from college anyway?" He tucked the crumpled-up sheets under his arm. "The one I think ended up at the CIA. You know, as a precaution."

I nodded. Maybe the government was quietly working on a Krinar vaccine that could make me immune to Vair? I'd gladly volunteer to test it.

"I think that'd be a good precaution," I said, though I doubted any human could protect us from Ks. "Especially if we risk going back to Vair's club tonight."

"Baby girl, I know we were both pretty spooked last night, but I feel better about the situation this morning after texting with Vair. I really don't get the sense that he intends to harm you. Think about it: he would've done it already. And besides"—Jay puffed his chest out, assuming a comical stance—"you'll be with me! What could possibly go wrong?"

I had to laugh. "What indeed."

"I mean, look," he said with a shrug, "maybe Vair wanting you at his club isn't about angry Krinar Council members *or* about Vair wanting to love you long time. Maybe it's as simple as Vair wanting to reignite the buzz about his club that your last article created."

"Maybe," I said doubtfully.

"It's just possible that not all vegan, bloodsucking alien overlords are villains, right? Vair could simply be opportunistic and capitalist-minded—like everyone else in this city."

I snorted. "One can hope."

"Atta girl!" He reached down and chucked me under the chin. "Do you want"—he held the balled-up sheets out to me—"your K blankie back?"

"Ugh, my God." I rose from the couch, shoving a laughing Jay from my path. "I'm going to shower now."

"Good idea," he called after me. "Wash that alien stink out of your hair."

CHAPTER SIXTEEN

"You can't wear that."

"Why not?"

"You'll look like a young MILF who got lost on her way to PTA night."

I rolled my eyes and held up the next dress option in front of me. "This one?"

Jay made a retching sound. "Are you going to a wedding or a sex club? I've said it before, I don't believe in puce."

I groaned and fished the last of my dress options from my TJ Maxx shopping bag. "How about this?"

Jay made a "meh" noise and gave it a "so-so" hand gesture. "I need to see what it looks like on. My hunch is that if Diane von Fürstenberg and Tory Burch had a bastard lovechild who designed cheap, slutty wrap dresses for Bebe, that's about what we've got here."

I flung it onto the chair next to his bed and tossed my hands in defeat. "Well, I'm out of options."

"Because you insisted on shopping where there were no options."

Jay had wanted me to shop in some trendy place in his Soho neighborhood, saying he envisioned me "braving Vair's club wearing an edgy, slinky, minimalist, bodycon Helmut Lang-esque number"—a.k.a. something way too expensive for my budget.

And given the fact that the last time I'd gone to his club, Vair had torn the nicest clubbing dress I'd owned to shreds, along with my bra and panties, I was not about to spend half of my paycheck on a designer dress that might suffer the same fate.

So I'd purchased six dresses from TJ Maxx instead, and I planned to take them all back—ideally, even whichever one I wore tonight to the club if I could manage to hide the tags.

"Did you get in touch with your friend at the CIA?" I asked.

"No, but I confirmed with a mutual friend that he does work there, and I got his number and left him a message."

It was progress, I supposed, but not all that comforting, given that we'd be back at Vair's club in less than five hours. Anything could happen to us tonight, and no one would be the wiser.

"And while you were out making substandard dress selections, I brainstormed some K interview questions." Jay pulled his phone from his pocket. "Want to hear them?"

I really didn't. "Sure. Lay them on me," I said brightly anyway.

My stomach was in knots, and I'd barely eaten all day. I'd stopped by my apartment after shopping to pick up my makeup bag, a selection of shoes, and other necessities for getting ready at Jay's place, and the entire time I'd been there, I hadn't been able to shake the paranoia that I was being watched. It was nerve-racking to think I might never have a sense of privacy in my own home again.

Jay sat on the edge of his bed and read from his iPhone. "What are the Krinar's ultimate plans for us as a society?"

I made a face. "Pass. Reasonable question, but too vague and easy to dance around answering. Besides, they obviously don't want us to know all of their intentions. Highly doubtful we'll get any worthwhile answer out of a K to that one." I could already envision Vair deflecting such a question with humor and sexual innuendo. "Next?"

"Why intervene and insert yourselves into our society now if you've had the ability to do so for thousands of years? If you were concerned about the health of our planet, why didn't you come to its rescue sooner?"

"Exactly!" I nodded. "Why indeed? I like it, but Ks aren't likely to answer that one either. Maybe we should start with x-club-related questions and try to pepper others into the convo as we can?"

"We?" He shook his head. "Baby girl, I'm afraid you're on your own with this. I'm dying to interview a K, but Vair was clear about only you doing the interviewing at his club."

Naturally. "Fine. *I'll* start with x-club-related questions. Got any of those?"

"Do I evah," Jay sing-songed. "Here's one that I wrote for Vair: It's rumored that more and more humans are frequenting your x-club. Many humans have shared stories on online forums about how addictive the experience of being bitten and having their blood sucked by a Krinar alien is. Is drinking human blood equally addictive for a Krinar?"

"Nice. Definitely an important, key question." *Professionally and personally.* And it was possible Vair or other Ks would entertain that one and perhaps provide some response from which I'd be able to extract a half-truth or two.

"You'll like this next one for Vair even better. While the Krinar continue to preach the merits of veganism and have strong-armed the entire planet into a predominantly vegan lifestyle, you've established an exclusive club where Krinar may access the fresh blood of willing humans—because apparently, the Krinar version of 'veganism' includes the blood of mammals? Care to explain that hypocrisy for the human public?"

I giggled and bounced in place on the balls of my feet. "I'll have to tone it down a bit, but I love it. What else?"

"How many other women have you been with in the past month?"

"Jay!"

"What?" He looked up from his phone with a devious grin. "Okay, so I admit that as I was writing these, they somehow became a bit more Vair and Amy hook-up specific than general K and x-clubber questions." His finger tapped and scrolled down the screen. "Let's see… I'll just skip over the next few," he said with a chuckle. "We can come back to the ones about how your blood tastes later."

"Ew! *Not* funny."

Jay got his laughter under control, cleared his throat, and continued. "I've heard that Krinar can be highly possessive. Does that mean that Krinar pair off and mate for life, like penguins, coyotes, and termites?"

I covered my face with my hands.

"What does it mean when a Krinar says that

they're going to 'take great care of someone' for *all eternity*? Is that like a Krinar euphemism for engaging in an extended sexual encounter?"

"Oh, my God." I flopped down onto the chair laden with my "substandard" dress choices. "I am not asking those questions. Let's move on. How about asking about their language? Or about how they're capable of understanding all of *our* languages so readily? Or about their technology and whether they ever plan to share any of those advances with us?"

Or if they intend to just keep using them against us—for control, intimidation, general spying, and the occasional sex tape compilation.

"Lame and lamer. Consider the venue, Amy. We're not meeting up at an Apple store. You're interviewing Vair and other horny Ks in a sex club. Besides, Vair said no boring, safe questions would be answered."

"What?" I jerked upright in my seat. "You talked with Vair while I was out?"

"Texted again."

"I want to see!" I demanded, reaching for the phone in his hands. "Show me the texts from this morning, too."

"I'd show you, but they've been erased."

"Bullshit." I jumped up and snatched the phone right out of his hands. "Why would you erase them?"

"I didn't. Vair did. Or *something* did. Because they disappeared seconds after I read them."

I scrolled through his recent text messages and confirmed that it was true.

"It's something with their technology, I'm sure."

"No doubt," I muttered, nodding absently. A new wave of anxiety curled in my gut as I heard my mother's voice in my head. *They wouldn't want to leave evidence behind of how they lured two unsuspecting human reporters to their beheading.*

I shook it off internally. I couldn't afford to go there. Jay seemed certain that we'd be safe tonight at Vair's club, and I had to trust his instincts on this. I knew that my own instincts were flawed—warped by years of my mother's constant fearmongering and "sky is falling" proselytization.

I'd seen a therapist about it in college. Being at school and away from my mom's influence for the first time had made me recognize just how poor my ability to judge the inherent danger of situations was. I'd learned in therapy that kids who were raised to fear everything in life were more likely to be victimized as adults—because being taught to see danger everywhere in the world, *including in places and situations where there was none*, left them with no reasonable gauge for identifying true danger when they were faced with it.

According to my therapist, when danger

becomes normalized, people stop hearing their intuition, until eventually they can't differentiate between the nebulous daily "sky is falling" threats and the "obvious to everyone but you creeper at the bar blatantly plotting to roofie your drink" threat.

My therapist had also cautioned me that sometimes those who were raised to see fear everywhere became subconscious thrill-seekers or adrenaline junkies in adulthood.

Knowing my instincts might be faulty, I relied on observation and fact as much as possible. And on the instincts of people I trusted.

Jay had been adamantly against the idea of me going to investigate and report on x-clubs at first. However, once we'd gotten in and were standing face to face with Vair, it was I who had become half-immobilized by fear and shock, while Jay had warmed to the situation, his instincts telling him that the threat was not as great as he'd initially feared. And he'd been right.

That time, my mother's voice warned in my head.

I handed Jay his phone and stood silently by the bed, lost in my thoughts.

"You want to text him for yourself and see?" he offered after a beat, awkwardly extending it back out to me.

"Oh, no. Definitely not."

"I could give you his number and you could use your own phone to text—"

"I'm good!" I snapped, then caught myself. "Sorry. Can we just veg out for a while? Watch a movie or something? I need to get my mind off things."

"Sure. I got *Men in Black, Alien vs. Predator, Independence Day*—"

"You're about to be strangled with a puce dress."

And as he erupted with laughter, I threw said dress at him.

CHAPTER SEVENTEEN

I OPTED TO WEAR THE VON-FÜRSTENBERG-BURCH bastard lovechild to Vair's club.

The perfectly symmetrical-faced K who'd confiscated and subsequently restored my boxes of office belongings the day before was waiting outside of Jay's building to collect us at exactly eleven p.m. He was driving a sleek but understated hybrid Lincoln Town Car. We learned that his name was Zyrnase.

Zyrnase seemed easygoing and friendly enough, chatting with us about how he liked living in the city, until Jay made the horrendous faux pas of asking if allergens were a common problem on Krina like they were on Earth—and followed it up with a joke about how "Zyrnase" sounded like the K might've been named after an antihistamine drug.

I cringed and slunk low in my seat as Zyrnase stoically informed us that no such ailment existed on Krina because allergens weren't the problem, our feeble human immune systems were. We fell silent for an uncomfortable length of time before Zyrnase activated the tinted glass divider and blocked us out entirely.

"Really? An antihistamine?"

"What? It was funny. Good clean K humor. Guy needs to lighten up," Jay grumbled under his breath. "Perfect facial structure gets dull fast when a person can't laugh at himself."

"I knew it!" I whisper-exclaimed. "You're into him."

"Duh. He's hot. *Was* hot. Before his personality disorder crashed our limo party. Which, by the way, sucks. There's no alcohol or even any snacks back here." Jay proceeded to rummage through all of the compartments he'd already ransacked. "You know, I get why drinking alcohol before getting your vein sucked might be a bad call, but how about offering your human suckees some frigging apple slices or mixed nuts? Even the shittiest blood bank offers crackers and cheap cookies to donors."

"Oh, God, you're nervous, aren't you? You're totally regretting coming tonight. Do you really think they're planning on biting us? I'll understand if you want to back out and not go in with me when we get there, okay? Zero judgment."

"What are you talking about? Of course I'm going in with you."

"You don't have to. I'm serious, Jay. This is my problem. *I* insisted on going there the first time. I'm the one who wrote the article that pissed off the Krinar Council."

"Well, *I'm* the best friend who insisted on coming with you that first time. And I had the hottest sex of my life that night, thank you very much. I'm also the same friend who negotiated this evening's reprise, and I'm not missing it."

"But, Jay—"

"But nothing." He pressed his fingers and thumb together in front of my face in the "zip it" gesture. "If you think I'm letting you hog all the hot aliens for yourself, you're blinder than those blinder glasses you're still wearing for no rational reason. Vair said I could come, and I'm going. End of discussion."

"Aw, Jay…" Blinking rapidly to stave off the tears stinging the backs of my eyes, I scooted closer and linked my arm through the crook of his. Leaning my head against his shoulder, I told him, "You're the best —you know that? Thank you."

The words sounded lame to my ears. They were grossly inadequate, given all that Jay was risking on my behalf. But I was never good at expressing such things. And I couldn't afford to get emotional tonight.

I knew Jay had always gotten that about me, because he never pushed emotional topics like some of my other friends did. Sure, he might tease me about having intimacy issues, but he always kept it light and playful. And he backed off whenever he sensed my discomfort. It was one of the qualities that made him such a remarkable friend.

"Yeah, yeah," he muttered. "So I've been told." He leaned his head on top of mine and gave my arm a squeeze.

We traveled for several blocks in contemplative silence.

"But for real," he broached as we passed through Greenwich Village, "why are you still wearing those glasses if your vision is worse with them on?"

I sighed and straightened in my seat, unlinking my arm from his. "Because it doesn't make sense. I've worn glasses since second grade. Vision doesn't just get better on its own."

"What if it did?"

"It's not possible."

"So you're still wearing them out of denial?"

"No, of course not. Look, maybe I just like the way they feel?" My statement had meandered into a question by the end.

Jay's blossoming lopsided grin said he wasn't buying it.

I couldn't blame him; I didn't either.

"What? They go with my dress!" I insisted with a giggle. "I like wearing glasses, okay? Can we drop it?"

He shrugged. "Whatever you say, baby girl." He gave me a wink. "Totally your business if you want to hide those gorgeous green eyes behind spectacles you can't see out of." His amused expression turned to puzzlement and his attention shifted to the window beside me when the car made a right turn. "Why is he turning here? This isn't the way we came last time."

I swiveled my head and saw that we'd turned down an alleyway. I didn't have the world's best sense of direction, but this definitely didn't look familiar to me. Granted, I couldn't see much between the darkness of the dimly lit alley and the blurriness my glasses created. "No," I said worriedly. "Doesn't seem like it."

My heart began to pound in my throat as all sorts of awful scenarios sprang to mind. I wished I'd been paying better attention to the route Zyrnase was taking.

"Well, I suppose it makes sense," Jay said as my panic was setting in. "He must be taking us through the super-secret high-profile celebrity entrance in the rear."

I forced out a nervous, half-assed chuckle. Jay took my hand in his and gave it a reassuring squeeze as our car came to a stop alongside the back of a nondescript, old brick building.

"What now?"

I'd barely whispered the question when, to my astonishment, the brick wall next to our car began to dissolve, creating an opening large enough for a car to drive through. And that's exactly where Zyrnase steered our car.

Darkness engulfed us as we drove straight down a ramp and into what appeared to be an underground tunnel. We proceeded to journey at slow speed with only the car's headlights to illuminate our way. I tried to remain calm, but after we'd driven for what felt like three whole blocks, I began to feel like I might hyperventilate.

"Okay, maybe I shouldn't have compared him to an antihistamine," Jay mused quietly next to me. I knew he was attempting to inject some humor into the tension-filled moment for my sake, but I heard the apprehension and alarm beneath his joking words as he asked, "Shall we jump out and make a run for it?"

"Somehow I doubt we'd get very far," I told him truthfully. "Let's not panic."

"Who's panicking?" he muttered. "No one in this car. You and I are not the panicking types."

I laughed so I wouldn't piss myself from fear.

My pulse jumped when our tires rolled to a stop once more in the middle of the darkened tunnel.

"On second thought—"

Jay's words were cut short as a reddish-purple light suddenly flooded the passenger cab. A large hole had opened up in the side of the tunnel where we'd stopped. Zyrnase drove us through it, and we found ourselves inside a subterranean parking garage.

About twenty feet later, we rolled to a final stop in a parking space marked with the letter "Z," and Zyrnase cut the engine.

"Jesus." Jay exhaled an exasperated sigh of relief as Zyrnase hopped out of the driver seat and made his way around the car to my door. "That was just a little over-the-fucking-top dramatic cloak-and-dagger, don't you think?"

It was an understatement. But I shushed Jay and quietly reminded him to play nice with the K as Zyrnase opened my door for me.

"Thanks… um… for the ride," I said as graciously as possible as I stepped out of the car, my legs as unsteady as my pulse after our unnerving journey. I extended my shaky hand to him, and his eyes widened strangely. Then he backed up a step, eyeing my hand like it was a poisonous snake.

"You're quite welcome," he said politely. *Without taking my outstretched hand.*

I dropped my arm and stepped aside.

When Jay climbed out of the car after me and held his hand out, Zyrnase shook it without hesitation.

Wow. Sexist much?

"Hey, thanks for the ride, man. Sorry about the bad joke before," Jay said.

Not for the first time, I marveled at how calm and collected my friend always managed to be—or at least seem.

"What joke?" Zyrnase responded, stone-faced. "I don't recall anything humorous." He shut the car door and turned his back on us. "Follow me."

"Um. Right. Hence the *bad* part—"

"Drop it," I told Jay with a sharp elbow jab to his ribs, and we followed after Zyrnase.

He led us through a hole he created in the parking garage wall. That took us down a long, gray hallway, and then through yet another hole he made in another wall, which led to another long hallway.

"Seriously, are we there yet? This is just overkill now," Jay complained loudly enough for Zyrnase to hear, prompting me to shush him again even though my stiletto-clad feet were beginning to agree.

I was also freezing, practically shivering in my

short, sleeveless wrap dress as we walked through the cold, barren hallways.

We were silent as we took a small elevator up two levels, before trailing after Zyrnase down another long, sterile, industrial-looking hallway.

"Hey," Jay piped up softly, leaning closer to me and slowing his pace. "Can't believe I forgot to tell you. I heard back from Stephen while you were getting ready. Slipped my mind as we were rushing out the door."

"Who?" I mouthed back.

"CIA friend," he mumbled covertly out of the side of his lips. "He wants to talk to you. Said your name is on a list."

"What?" I mouthed, aghast.

He nodded and then jerked his head in Zyrnase's direction, murmuring, "Let's talk about it tomorrow."

"My name is on a list? What kind of list?"

Jay's eyes flashed in warning, but he shook his head and whispered back, "No idea. Said it was classified."

"Are you serious?"

"Later," he insisted, pressing his forefinger to his lips.

I shut up, but my mind was whirling.

How could I have gotten onto a classified government list?

We turned a corner at the end of the hallway, and my heart tripped when I spied Vair standing there, not more than twenty feet away—his tall, commanding, bronzed presence a thing of surreal beauty that sent a purely feminine thrill through me.

"It's nice to see you again, little human," he said. "Welcome back to my club."

CHAPTER EIGHTEEN

I should've been insulted by his "little human" remark. But his tone was so warm, and the enchanted look he was giving me made it seem like the greatest of compliments.

"Hi."

I couldn't think of anything more eloquent to say as I stood there staring at him—feeling the strain in my cheeks from the goofy grin that had spread, unbidden, across my face. I knew exactly which grin it was, too. It was the same one found in every one of my elementary school photos—before I'd learned with age and good sense how to rein it in and smile like a normal person.

It was my overly excited, unrestrained smile, and it had absolutely no business staging an appearance now—in front of the mocking, domineering, sexy bastard of an alien who had used incriminating sex tape footage to blackmail me into coming to his x-club tonight.

As Vair walked toward me, it became easier to control my exuberant grin, while harder to will the rest of my features into a semblance of something subdued and appropriate. With each graceful step he took in my direction, his sheer size and otherworldly magnetism had me feeling torn between turning around and fleeing, and leaping into his arms to climb him like a tree.

Even at a distance, and with me wearing my blurred-vision glasses, those dark brown eyes of his were drawing me into their infinite depths, making me forget all the reasons I hadn't wanted to come to his club tonight—all the reasons that he was a danger to me and to the human race.

In that moment, there was only the chemistry between us: a force that defied logic and reason, scoffed at the inherent differences between our species, and disregarded the complications of our interplanetary politics.

"Hey, man. Great to see you again." Jay stepped directly in front of me, obstructing Vair's path in what was at once the most badass and foolishly suicidal best-friend cock-blocking move ever. "Thanks for having us back to your club."

I had completely forgotten that Jay and Zyrnase were even standing in the hallway with us.

Jay's height and musculature may have been impressive for a human male, but Vair's Krinar physique dwarfed his easily. And Vair did not appear happy with Jay for interrupting our moment. His mercurial dark eyes had gone from warm and effusive as they'd stared at me to possessive and forbidding as they'd narrowed on Jay.

My concern for my friend prompted me to find my voice at last. "Vair, you remember my best *friend,* Jay," I said, putting added emphasis on the "friend" part.

His jaw tight, an imitation of a smile on his lips, Vair clapped Jay none too gently on the shoulder and bit out a curt welcome, before bodily steering my best friend aside, out of his way.

My grade-school grin came back, accompanied by the most embarrassing schoolgirl blush, as Vair stood directly in front of me—his imposing presence once again blocking out all else, the heat emanating from his powerful body burning straight through every part of me.

"Hi," I said stupidly again.

He laughed softly and parroted, "Hi."

He took both of my trembling hands in his, warming them and chasing away the last of my fear. Replacing it with a different brand of excitement as he brought each of my hands to his lips, one after the other, depositing scalding kisses that made me regret I hadn't stashed an extra pair of panties into the tiny evening bag hanging from my shoulder.

"You look very nice, Amy." His deep, lulling voice was hypnotic as his lips brushed across the sensitive skin of my knuckles. "It's good to have you here."

My whole body came alive at his slightest touch, my muscles tightening with anticipation and my insides turning to liquid fire. My eyes fluttered shut and I swayed closer, breathing in his scent like the xenophile that I was for him.

"I'm glad you were brave enough to come tonight, darling."

The familiar words he'd used in my dream the night before proved to be the figurative bucket of ice water I needed.

My eyes flew open as it hit me: I had been right. Vair *had* visited me inside Jay's condo last night. That hadn't been a dream.

I gave myself a mental slap.

What the fuck was wrong with me?

I yanked my hands from his grasp. He relinquished them with a frown, and I took a step back, putting much-needed space between us.

I'd been standing there *blushing*. Gazing into Vair's eyes, stealing whiffs of his heavenly K scent, acting as if we were a couple out on our second date, when this was the same mocking, stalking, wall-dissolving-and-entering, videotaping, blackmailing K who was a threat to both my career and my life.

"Brave?" Jay interjected with a laugh, stepping up to my rescue when I remained at a loss for words. "Vair, man, no offense, but Amy and I have been to waaay crazier sex clubs than yours."

I nearly choked on my own spit as my head whipped in my friend's direction. Either Jay was the bravest person I knew or he seriously had a death wish.

"Is that right?" Vair said softly.

"Yeah." Jay shrugged, looking unperturbed by the cold promise of murder that had bled into the K's tone. "We're reporters, as you know. Goes with the territory."

I cringed internally.

Oblivious, my coworker proceeded to double-down on his sex-clubbing boast, beaming as he confided with a chuckle, "Since Amy and I are the youngest and best-looking journalists at *The Herald*, we're the logical choice to go undercover to research the most exclusive sex clubs in the city." He gave another shrug. "When duty calls," he sing-songed. "So here we are. No longer undercover and ready to roll whenever you are with those interview questions you promised you'd allow Amy."

I gulped. Vair was looking at Jay like he might end my friend on the spot.

But then Vair smiled thinly and responded with a nonchalant, "Of course. And I'm happy to oblige. But first, I think you should have a look around and maybe spend some time behind the bar to gain a better sense of some of the inner workings of our club—see how it compares to all the others you've been to."

He wanted us to bartend?

"Awesome," Jay agreed with enthusiasm. "Lead the way."

"I'm afraid I have other business and guests to attend to for most of the night. Zyrnase will show you around."

I tried to ignore the abrupt sense of disappointment—not to mention, anxiety—that spiked in me at the prospect of not actually spending time with Vair while in his club tonight.

If my dejection showed on my face, Vair didn't see it. Because he wasn't looking at me—adding another unwelcome layer of rejection to round out this unsettling turn of events. Only yesterday, Vair had professed in the limo that he *needed* me back at his club. He'd expressed to Jay that we would be here under his protection. Now he was simply casting us out on our own?

Vair's focus was on Zyrnase as he directed, "Take

them to the upstairs bar, and see that Tauce looks after them. Let him know who she is, and tell him I said she was free to interview him." He spared only the briefest glance in my direction as he said this. "I'll send Shalee to speak with her as well, when she's available."

Zyrnase nodded, but I got the sense he wasn't exactly thrilled with what seemed to me like a newly hatched arrangement. And I couldn't shake the suspicion that we were about to be thrown to the wolves.

"Wait. You don't need to be present for her interview with this Tauce guy?" Jay asked. "Or Shalee?"

Vair smiled. "I'm sure Tauce and Shalee will manage fine without me."

"But I thought you were concerned about Amy's protect—"

"It's fine," I cut Jay off. "I'll be fine."

I hoped.

I wasn't about to let Vair think that I needed or wanted him to babysit me at his club. And I was perfectly capable of interviewing Ks on my own, without his supervision—or interference.

Vair smiled at me—a predator's grin—his teeth gleaming white within his smoothly sculpted, bronzed face. "Of course you will be."

He stepped closer and grasped me by both

shoulders, the heat of his palms branding my bare skin as he invaded my personal space. His lips ghosted over my cheek before dipping to my ear to whisper, "I'm counting on you to play nice with the other aliens, darling. Don't disappoint me."

The hell?

What did that mean?

Vair traded quick words in his own language with Zyrnase as he backed away from me, a sexy, disarming grin gracing his perfect face.

When Vair was gone and we were continuing down yet *another* hallway several safe paces behind Zyrnase, I socked Jay in the bicep and hissed in his ear, "Quit antagonizing Ks!"

"Me? You started it."

"What did I do?"

"Girl, you've got to get your lust under control around Vair. You can't just look at a guy like that."

Crap. "Like what? How was I looking at him?"

"Like you wanted to make alien babies with him."

"I did not."

"Did so. And like make them right there in the hallway in front of me and Zyrnase."

"You were imagining things."

He laughed. "Well, I wasn't the only one imagining things. Pretty sure Vair was about to take you up on your unspoken offer before I stepped in between you two."

"Yeah, well… thanks for that. I appreciate it. But it was foolish and dangerous. Which reminds me…" I punched his arm again. "Are you trying to get yourself killed boasting about our fabricated sex-clubbing experience?"

"Oh, come on, it was great. And now we know that Krinar can get butthurt just like humans can. I'm thinking of making that the topic of *my* K exposé."

∼

We entered the upstairs bar at Vair's x-club through one final hole in the last hallway. The multicolored lights that greeted us brought back memories of our first visit, as did the ethereal, weeping musical undertones of some mysterious instrument playing amid the sharper vibrations and pulsing background beat.

The bar area looked similar to the one we'd been in before, but it was definitely not the same space, making me wonder just how large the entire club was. This room was a little smaller than the one we'd been in during our first visit, but with more intimate lounge seating areas featuring privacy drapes along the walls rather than the circular tables that had served as bars. The dance floor here was slightly elevated, and there was a large, futuristic-looking circular half-bar composed of what appeared to be metal and white molded glass lit from within.

The Krinar were easy to spot in the room, their superior height, bronzed skin, and stunning supermodel attributes setting them apart from even the most beautiful of the humans present on the dance floor. As before, the Ks were dressed in simplistic, light-colored clothing that accentuated their healthy-looking, tanned skin, and in fabrics that seemed to conform to their bodies in a way that emphasized their graceful, impressive physiques—causing me to feel a moment of inadequacy and regret over my outfit selection as I covertly wiped my damp palms on the skirt of my dress.

After a month of obsessing over my last visit, I was officially back inside Vair's x-club. I was just beginning to get my nerves under control and my game face on when a ruckus started on the dance floor.

"I told you not to come back here!"

CHAPTER NINETEEN

The music cut off and the lights brightened, illuminating the kerfuffle that had erupted.

An enormous Krinar male with a completely shaved head and striking greenish-yellow eyes was holding a tall, clean-cut-looking young human man up by his throat with one hand. As huge as Vair was, this bald K looked even bigger—maybe a few inches taller and packing another thirty pounds of muscle.

If I'd noticed him on the street in broad daylight carrying a bag of groceries, I might've been alarmed enough to walk briskly in the opposite direction. Seeing him holding a struggling human in the air with ease was positively terrifying.

"Who *the cusack* let this guy in here again?" the scary K demanded. His eyes—more yellow than green now—casually scanned the room in accusation before returning to regard the man in his grasp with renewed disdain. "Last call. Any Krinar want to claim him?"

Those stark yellow eyes, set amid perfectly symmetrical, sharp features, and so pronounced against his deeply tanned skin, reflected zero compassion for the victim in his grasp, who was turning purple for lack of air and clutching desperately at the massive hand around his throat.

And I mean zero.

I tugged Jay's elbow. "We have to do something."

"I know, but what?" he whispered, his face pale. "Get ourselves killed?"

"Tauce won't kill him," Zyrnase reassured us, his voice devoid of concern.

That was Tauce? The K Vair had elected to "look after us" was this crazy-eyed killer alien choking a man to death in the middle of a dance floor?

Thrown to the wolves, indeed.

"Are you shitting me?" Jay exclaimed. "That's the guy she's supposed to interview? *Alone?* Where's Vair? I want to talk to him."

"There's no need for that. Tauce!"

At Zyrnase's sharply spoken call, the giant K let the poor human man drop to the floor in a semiconscious heap.

"Don't come back," Tauce coldly told the man, who was now twitching and coughing on the ground, holding his throat as he struggled to take in air again.

The K's words held the promise of certain death should the man be foolish enough to disobey.

But why?

What on earth had the man done? He didn't look much older than early to mid-twenties. And he was obviously no match for a K. What could possibly have gone down to warrant such treatment?

Pushing my fear of the yellow-eyed K aside, I took a step forward as Jay and Zyrnase started arguing over Vair's choice of babysitter and interviewee for me.

Other Ks came and removed the human man from the dance floor, the lights dimmed, and the music resumed as Tauce stomped off, heading over to the bar, a disgusted, angry look still etched on his face. Which, for all I knew, might've been his normal expression.

My heart fluttered in my throat as I took a second step, and then another.

I told myself it was because I was curious. That it was simply the reporter in me driven to know the facts of the situation—to understand what a human could've possibly done at an alien sex club to deserve to be attacked and threatened in the way I'd just witnessed.

It wasn't because I felt challenged by Vair's "play

nice with the other aliens" remark, or because I wanted to show Vair that I was brave enough to confront whatever scary alien dares he was willing to dish out.

And it certainly wasn't because his influence called to the subconscious thrill-seeking adrenaline junkie in me who lacked the good judgment to gauge true danger when faced with it. This was about getting the facts straight and having my interview questions answered by a K for my next article.

Summoning all of my nerve, I cautiously ambled closer until I was standing in front of the great beast of a K who was angrily stewing behind the bar. He glanced up at my approach and smiled. *And somehow managed to look even more frightening when he did.*

"Well, hell-o there, sweetness." Lascivious green eyes had my wrap dress off in seconds flat. "I'm Tauce." He reached across the lit bar between us, offering me his ginormous throat-choking hand. "First time at the club?"

"Yieeeccch!" Zyrnase released a bizarre-sounding distress cry from behind me, where he'd been arguing with Jay. "She's Vair's human!"

Tauce withdrew his hand at unnatural speed, exclaiming something that sounded like "fuck," but with more syllables. His eyes were wide and disbelieving as they looked over my shoulder in Jay and Zyrnase's direction. "Charl?" he asked.

"Uh, no, name's Jay." Jay rushed forward to stand protectively next to me. He extended his hand to Tauce. "I'm assuming you already know Zyrnase?"

Tauce didn't take Jay's hand. The scornful look he leveled at my friend made me like the K even less than I had ten seconds ago. "I was referring to the lady," he said, his wide, square jaw jutting in my direction.

"Her name's not Charl, either," Jay told him. "It's Amy."

Tauce's eyes turned a shade that was almost neon yellow as his annoyed glare transferred from Jay to Zyrnase. "Don't even say it, Z. Not tonight."

"Vair wants you to look after them."

"Aw, *cusack!*"

I decided "cusack" must be the Krinar equivalent of "fuck"—or something along those lines. In any case, it wasn't a happy word.

Zyrnase and Tauce argued in Krinar. It didn't last long, and I knew Tauce had lost his case when he scrubbed an enormous hand over his face and groused "cusack" three times in rapid succession.

∽

ZYRNASE LEFT US IN TAUCE'S CAPABLE KILLER HANDS. Tauce spent the better part of the first twenty minutes with us serving drinks and ignoring our presence as we stood idly behind the bar, keeping out of his way as much as possible.

When he wasn't procuring a beverage for someone, he was tracing things into his palm with his pointer finger—usually with his nostrils flared and his upper lip curled in contempt. Sometimes he appeared to be reading things from his forearm. I couldn't decide if he was still pouting over his missed homicide opportunity on the dance floor, or if all his emo alien ire was for us.

Jay attempted to engage him in conversation, but to no avail. It wasn't until we decided to leave him sulking by himself in favor of exploring the room on our own that he chose to interact—*to stop us.*

He corralled us back behind the bar, and let it be known that we were not to leave his presence. It became clear that Vair had designated Tauce as our bodyguard-slash-babysitter—a revelation that was somewhat reassuring in the sense that it meant Vair seemingly did want to keep us safe while we were in his club. And yet it was also disappointing.

Hanging out with Grumpy K while he was working and moping was very anticlimactic after the amount of speculating and stressing that Jay and I had done in the past twenty-four hours.

"We walked through twenty wall dissolves for this?" Jay complained.

He pointed out that if we had to watch angry

paint dry for the rest of the night, we had better start drinking. Unfortunately, the x-club bar wasn't stocked with Jay's usual vodka shots. In fact, it wasn't stocked at all—it was literally an empty bar.

Tauce would simply wave his hand or ask for a certain drink, and it would appear—rising up from hidden compartments below the white glass surface of the bar. Making his "bartender" role seem a tad superfluous, in my opinion.

The exotic purple fruit juice mixed with mild alcohol that Vair had given me the last time I'd been here seemed to be the most popular choice for the human clubgoers. Jay began referring to it as an "alien Shirley Temple" after he consumed two glasses and failed to catch a buzz.

"I think they do it on purpose," Jay said, noisily slurping down the remains of his second glass in vain while Tauce brooded and kept watch over us from the other end of the bar.

"Do what?"

"Serve such mild, benign drinks that after a while, you're so desperate to catch a high you'll willingly sign up for a vein tapping by any K available. Makes sense, right?"

I laughed and shook my head. "I don't know. I'm still on my first glass, and I can feel the alcohol a little. I definitely feel something… like some kind of warmth or energy flowing through me. Maybe it's just the music." Or my waning adrenaline rush.

"I think it's Tauce's laser eyes burning into your rear. Seriously, I'm about to throw down in your honor if he doesn't quit staring."

"Shhh, keep it down; he'll hear you."

"That's the point. I'll tell you, the very last thing I expected was to be bored tonight." Jay set his empty glass onto the bar. "It's literally the only scenario I never contemplated in coming here."

I had to agree. But it felt wrong to be disappointed about that. We should've been relieved to be bored.

"Hey, at least we're safe," I reminded Jay. "That's the most important thing. This is a way better outcome than any other scenario."

"Speak for yourself. Not all of us value safety above all else in life, baby girl." Jay waved his hand over the top of his glass the way we'd seen Tauce do.

Nothing happened. When Tauce had done it, the bar would open up and pull the glass down below the surface.

"I command you to take the glass away," Jay intoned in a ridiculous voice, loudly enough to garner a scowl from Tauce.

"Cut it out. He'll think we're making fun."

"Good. Vair implied we'd get to work the bar. He said we'd get to look around and gain a better sense of the inner workings of his club. Nothing we've done with Tauce so far remotely qualifies." Jay shouted the last part in Tauce's direction. "He also said we'd get to interview Tauce, but the guy won't even speak with us. He just stands there pretending to doodle on his palm and read things from his forearm."

I swore I could hear Tauce's teeth gnashing from ten feet away as Jay continued his tirade. The K looked like he was angry-tracing on his palm now.

"And anytime another K or human tries to interact with us, anti-soc baldie over there scares them away. Vair's treating us like children, Amy. Either we get some real drinks and a real interview with a K, or I say we get out of here."

Right. Like it was that easy. Vair was up to something with this arrangement; I just couldn't figure out what. In the interim, I needed to calm Jay down and get him to shut the hell up before he pushed our alien babysitter too far.

But then Jay stopped talking on his own, riveted by the sight of a statuesque brunette K approaching the bar.

Her glossy, shoulder-length hair fell in loose, natural waves, and she was wearing a body-hugging white, short, asymmetrical tank dress that was the perfect, effortless marriage of casual sexy and haute couture chic. Her gaze paused briefly as it swept over Jay before meeting mine. She smiled and extended her hand to me, and I noticed how her brown eyes had striking shades of amber in them.

"I'm Shalee."

I took Shalee's proffered hand and gave it a firm shake. Tauce made no attempt to stop me.

"Nice to meet you. I'm Amy."

"I know. I work very closely with Vair. It's a pleasure to meet you, Amy."

My heart sped up and something in my gut twisted at her words, even as I kept a pleasant smile on my face. "Oh? How nice. For how long?"

I hadn't meant to voice that question, but seeing as I couldn't take it back, I decided to expand on it. "What kind of work? What do you do with him?"

Are you sleeping with him?

"Research." She canted her head, studying me with squinted eyes as the right side of her mouth curved up. "Mostly."

Bitch.

"I'm Jay." My best friend thrust his hand forward, practically shouldering me out of his way to get directly in front of Shalee.

I took the hint and stepped aside.

Shalee's smile widened. "Hi, Jay." She took his hand, and I watched as normally suave, socially sophisticated Jay just stood there, speechless, staring at Vair's gorgeous coworker like he might drool on himself at any moment.

"We're not together," he finally spoke up with a nod in my direction. "In case… in case you were wondering." He was still holding her hand.

"I know."

"This is going to sound like the world's cheesiest pick-up line," Jay began, then paused to catch his breath.

I thought about shoving him back out of the way to save him from himself, but I didn't know if I'd be able to break the hold he had on Shalee's hand. And some small, evil part of me did want to hear Jay's cheesiest pick-up line for humor's sake.

"I swear I had a dream about you last night," Jay confessed in total sincerity.

Lordy.

Shalee's brow lifted—in apparent genuine interest, too, not in a "you've got to be kidding me" way. "Really? What were we doing?"

She wasn't serious, was she? She seemed way too smart to fall for that. Had they never heard that tired line on Krina?

"In my dream, you were a nurse." Jay cleared his throat. "And you made… a house call."

I coughed. Loudly. But Jay didn't look away from Shalee to catch my signal.

"You don't say?" She sounded legit intrigued.

There was no way she was going for this. "What was the treatment?"

"You gave me some kind of hangover prevention medicine."

She bit her lip, assessing him with a sexy smile. "Did it work?"

This was like watching bad porn. She *had* to be messing with him.

He nodded. *And blushed.* I had never seen my friend blush before.

"Very well, actually." He gestured to the dance floor. "Would you like to—?"

"Yes," she answered. "I would."

No way.

She looked to me. "You don't mind if I borrow him for a bit, do you?"

Yeah, I did, actually. I pinched Jay's elbow to gain his attention. He didn't even flinch. It was as if he was hypnotized by Shalee's face.

"Oh, well, I think Tauce wants us to stay—"

"Take him," Tauce intervened, shutting me down. "It's fine."

CHAPTER TWENTY

I LOST SIGHT OF JAY AND SHALEE AFTER THEIR SECOND dance, when they moved to the lounge seating area along the wall and drew the privacy curtains. From the way they'd been all over one another on the dance floor, I didn't expect that I'd see either of them again very soon.

It felt uncannily like the last time I'd been here, when Jay had abandoned me for Alien Barbie Shira, only worse, because Vair wasn't by my side. And Jay's departure and subsequent love fest on the dance floor with Shalee had made Vair's absence feel all the more pronounced.

It had also made hanging out alone with Tauce nearly unbearable.

But at least I was safe, I reminded myself.

Safety was key.

I'd given in and taken to wearing my glasses on top of my head instead of over my eyes in order to scan the crowd and people-watch rather than observe Tauce staring at his own hand. I was beginning to come to terms with the fact that I really couldn't see well with my eyewear on anymore.

Another thirty minutes and an "alien Shirley Temple" later, my stilettos were killing me. My night was going nowhere fast and I had nothing to lose, so I decided to try and throw out a few of the interview questions Jay had come up with.

"Hey, so um, Vair said… he said that I could interview you. Is that… is that okay?"

Tauce didn't react. He didn't even twitch an eyelash. He just stood there, staring me down.

I fidgeted on my feet, tucking my hair behind my ear. "So what are the Krinar's ultimate plans for us as a society?"

I'd known it was a bad question. Tauce confirmed it.

His eyes widened. Then he slow-blinked. "You do this for a living? And they *pay* you?"

Ass.

Fine. "What's with pushing veganism on the planet when you're all here getting high on human blood? That hardly qualifies as a vegan diet."

He made a soft grunting noise and pinched the bridge of his nose, shaking his head.

Fuck.

"How long have you worked here?"

He gave me his back.

Not even that one he'd answer?

"How do you like living in New York City?" I called after him as he walked to the other end of the bar.

"Hi, Tauce." A striking blond woman strolled up to where he had gone to ignore me and leaned across the bar, spilling ample boobage from her ultra-sexy, barely-there dress. "Will I see you in the basement later?"

I thought she might be a Krinar at first, but then I saw that she was too short. As I studied her closer, I realized she looked vaguely familiar, but I knew I didn't know her.

As I watched Tauce's apathetic response to her flirting, it hit me where I'd seen her before: gracing the covers of tabloids in the supermarket checkout line. She was a well-known soap opera star who'd been on the same show for ages. I was pretty sure she'd won numerous Daytime Emmy Awards. I couldn't think of her name, though, as I'd never seen the popular show she was on.

She gave up trying to entice him and strutted off when Tauce ignored her boobs in favor of drawing on his palm with his finger in that weird way he'd been doing.

I rushed over to him once she was gone. "Oh, my God. Was that—"

"Yes," Tauce cut me off with an eye roll. "It was. Yes, she's some kind of... television personality." He said it like it was the dumbest job a person could have, or be impressed by. "All the humans ask that when she comes in."

It was reassuring to know I was just like every dumb human Tauce encountered in Vair's club. "She comes here a lot?"

He shrugged, and I thought that he was done with the conversation. But after a beat, he offered up: "She's a nymphomaniac; likes a K in every hole when she comes here. I enjoy taking her in the ass."

Alrighty. It was my turn to slow-blink.

I resisted. Because this was a Tauce breakthrough. Maybe he would talk if the topic was sex?

"Are you a polyamorous society on Krina?"

His yellow-green eyes raked me up and down. "We like to have sex. Sometimes in groups. More often in pairs."

Interesting. *Which did Vair prefer?*

"We don't suffer the prudish social constraints that plague your society."

"Plague?" I had to giggle. I was nearly giddy with excitement that he was finally engaging with me and answering my questions. "That's a tad dramatic."

He gave me his best stone-faced Tauce look in reply.

Okay, then. "Do Krinar ever pair off for life? You know, get married? Or something similar to that? Like humans do?"

He made a face like he'd just smelled something awful. "If they're unlucky."

Right. And I'd bet my left kidney the K who ended up saddled with Tauce for life would consider herself the unlucky one in that arrangement.

"So is it more of a societal arrangement then? Not because the Krinar pair wants to?"

"No. They do it because they want to." He looked down at his palm, becoming distracted with whatever he was seeing there.

I was losing him. I needed to steer the conversation back to sex.

"I overheard the blond actress ask whether she'd be seeing you in the basement later. Is that where you've, um… hooked up with her before?"

Tauce looked up from his palm, his brow arched in amusement. "Hooked up? You mean fucked?" He shook his head. "I can't believe you're Vair's human."

"And what does that mean?" I failed to keep the affront I felt at his tone from my voice. Zyrnase had referred to me in those same terms when I'd been introduced to Tauce. I hadn't wanted to read into it or analyze its meaning too closely at the time. "Do you mean I'm Vair's human guest when you say that?" I asked hopefully.

He smirked. Some guys managed to pull off "cocky-sexy" when they smirked; Tauce just looked like a dick.

"No, little reporter, it means you're Vair's property. It means that he owns you."

I forced a breath as I felt the blood draining from my face.

Don't panic, don't panic. It's not what it sounds like he's saying.

"You mean while I'm here at his club? Like in an erotic power-exchange kind of deal? Dom and sub stuff? Because I haven't—I didn't agree to do anything… like that…" I trailed off, swallowing hard at the nasty look of amusement that spread across Tauce's features.

He bent his head closer to mine, his penetrating yellow-green eyes staring me down. "Ks don't need permission from humans," he informed me in a cold whisper. "We take what we want. We keep what we claim as ours."

My face burned with indignation. "No one owns me, Tauce."

He laughed. His laughter came off even worse on the bastard scale than his smirk.

Recognizing the futility of continuing to argue

this point with him given my present predicament, I decided to change the subject.

"So what was with that guy earlier on the dance floor?" I shifted my glasses back down over my eyes, not wanting to see any more than I had to of Tauce's face. "What happened?"

"He was warned not to come back here."

"Yeah, I kind of caught that from your exchange. But why? What did he do to get banned from the club?"

Not surprisingly, I was met with blurry stone-faced Tauce in response, followed by him ignoring me to fiddle with his palm.

"What is up with the damn palm business, already?" I was beyond over it.

His head jerked up at my tone. "I'm working," he said, as if stating the obvious.

"You're working? On your palm?"

"Yes."

"I'm sorry." I shook my head. "I'm not following. How is that working?"

"The same way you humans work on your cellular devices."

"You have a tiny phone in your hand? Where?" I moved closer, grabbing for his hand as curiosity got the better of me.

He pulled back before I could touch him. "Not a phone. And it's not for your human eyes to see."

Ah. Right. The 'ole *Emperor's New Clothes* deal—a K device that was invisible to unfit humans. Made total sense within their technologically advanced world of dissolving walls.

It was the perfect segue to broach the topic of K technology and to ask Tauce whether the Krinar ever planned to share any of their advances with us. But instead, I found myself asking, "You got anything stronger to drink in this place?"

I set my glasses back atop my head and rubbed my sore eyes.

What I really wanted to ask was what time my shift ended tonight. Because that's exactly what this felt like: working a shift at a shitty clock-watching job where you lost hours of your life talking to people you'd never willingly engage with had you not been coworkers.

"Not for you," Tauce replied.

I nodded, putting my glasses back in place. "Figures."

"How about a change of scenery instead?" Tauce suggested.

"Yes!" I agreed, a little too enthusiastically. "I mean, yeah, that'd be great. I'd love to tour other parts of the club."

I pushed my glasses up again so that I could see his face and gauge his sincerity, but he was busy messing with his stupid palm once more. When he was done, he glanced up and gave me a stoic, "Come with me. I need to work the downstairs bar now."

~

We walked through a hole Tauce made in the wall behind the bar area, down a surprisingly short, dark hallway, and into a small elevator.

I felt a little anxious about leaving Jay behind in the upstairs bar, but I had a feeling he'd be safe with Shalee. And I wouldn't be gone long, I rationalized—even though I had no idea how long Tauce was supposed to work this downstairs bar we were headed to.

When the elevator opened at the basement level, I was expecting to find a hallway or at the very least another wall that Tauce would need to dissolve before we reached our final destination. But instead, the doors opened and we were thrust smack-dab into the middle of a busy club scene.

A scene that I was woefully unprepared for.

People—and aliens—were having sex. *Everywhere.* In cages suspended from the ceiling, in cages on the ground, on the dance floor, against the wall —*suspended by chains in some cases.*

A woman was being eaten out on a table mere feet from where we were standing!

My mouth went dry as I met Tauce's smug eyes. He was clearly enjoying my discomfort.

"I'd rather work the bar upstairs," I managed to say.

He gave me a look that said I wasn't getting anything I wanted—at least not from him.

"I want to speak with Vair about this."

He smirked. "You're in luck. Vair's the reason you're down here. Follow me."

He took off at an easy stride, and I was torn between not wanting to be left alone in this triple-X basement bar scene and not wanting to follow and see how much worse it might get. When I didn't immediately follow, he turned around and made a hissing sound at me.

An actual. Hissing. Sound.

Oh, my God. This guy. I rolled my eyes and bit my lip to keep from telling him to *cusack* the hell off.

He was in front of me in a blink, with that perpetually irate, constipated-looking expression that I'd privately dubbed "resting Tauce face" during the hour and forty-three minutes I'd endured with him.

"Do you not understand the word *follow*, human?"

"Oh, was that what you said? I couldn't hear you over the music and screaming down here."

His hiss morphed into a growl. Then he seemed to make an attempt to compose himself.

"Listen, *Amy...*" He addressed me by my name for the very first time, and managed to make it sound like a foul disease he didn't want to contract. "Someone's liable to suck and fuck you and ask questions later if you don't stick close to me down here."

He had me at "suck."

I held my palm up in surrender. "Got it. Lead the way. I'll *follow.*"

I stuck close to Tauce as he wove a path through the basement of Sodom and Gomorrah. As horrified as I was by the sights and sounds that surrounded me, I found myself unwittingly turned on by some of them as well.

Any fledgling hope I'd quietly harbored about Vair not being into the really kinky stuff was squashed as we passed by naked people gagged and bound to sex furniture and tied to x-shaped Saint Andrew's crosses.

Why, oh why hadn't I kept my mouth shut and stayed upstairs in the safe bar?

My system was on overload, my shaky fingers continuously sliding my glasses up and down between the bridge of my nose and the tip, torn between wanting to see and not wanting to know.

I was so disoriented I barely noticed my steps,

much less paid attention to where we were going, and before I knew it, I'd walked through an opening in a wall that Tauce had made. In front of me was the famous blond actress from the bar upstairs—engaged in a scene I could've gladly gone my whole life not knowing about.

CHAPTER TWENTY-ONE

Multiple men—Krinar—were touching her.

And were inside her.

At once.

Others were waiting their turn. And judging by the euphoric, inhuman sounds coming out of her, the beautiful Emmy award-winning actress was one hundred percent down with this. Then again, they'd likely bitten her, and as Jay had said, a bite from a K was like the most potent drug.

Tauce nudged me from behind and I stumble-entered the room—having tripped over my own slack jaw as I tried to block out the sounds I was hearing. To un-see what I was witnessing.

Vair was seated in an elevated white lounge chair at the edge of the bed. His chair appeared to be floating above the floor—in the same manner the circular platform bed was doing. Upon my clumsy entrance, his floating chair swiveled in my direction. He looked like the Greek god Dionysus himself, sitting on his throne, all dark and gorgeous, casually observing the orgy before him. *Buck-naked.*

I spun on my heel, intending to flee back upstairs to the bar, only to find Tauce already gone and the opening in the wall I'd come through sealed off.

"Come, now, don't be shy." Vair's arms were encircling me from behind in an instant, his throaty laughter just loud enough to be heard above the panicked blood roaring in my ears and the woman having an orgasm behind me, as he half-dragged, half-carried me over to the chair he'd vacated. "I want you to observe and take notes for me."

Take notes?

He pulled me straight into his lap as he reseated himself, his arm wrapping firmly around my waist so that I couldn't have moved an inch even if I hadn't been rendered stiff from shock. "This is your opportunity to get answers. You like observing and reporting facts, remember?"

He was mocking me again. But I was too scared shitless to care. I was in his naked lap in a sealed room where an alien orgy was taking place.

My fight reflex belatedly kicked in, and I struggled wildly against him. "No, I can't! I'm not wired like that. I don't do group sex. Please, I'm a terrible multitasker!"

"Shh-shh—calm down." His palm clamped over my mouth. "I asked you to observe and take notes." The genuine annoyance in his voice did more to soothe me than his actual words. He tipped my head back at an awkward angle until I found myself staring up into his glaring countenance. "No one touches you but me, little human. Understand?"

His proclamation was delivered in a tone that was downright grumpy—nasty even. "Little human" falling from the twisted line of his angry lips sounded more like a slight than the endearment it had seemed to me earlier. So it made no sense when my heart warmed at his words and the paralyzing fear I'd felt abruptly abated.

No one touched me but him. I could get on board with that—for the moment, at least.

His fingers flexed, biting into the hollow planes below my cheekbones, silently demanding my response. I nodded against his palm and his eyes softened, if not his mouth.

Removing his hand, he yanked me upright in his lap and dropped an odd-looking electronic notepad into my sweaty hands. It was slightly larger than my phone, but lighter. I dazedly listened to his brusque instructions as he relayed the features, showing me how I could take notes manually or via the recorder feature.

Oh, my God, he was serious about me taking notes?

Fine, I could do this. I was a *reporter*. Taking orgy notes was better than being expected to participate in one.

I swallowed and forced my eyes up from the electronic device in my hands to the group of perfectly formed naked male bodies undulating and thrusting directly in front of me.

Just disconnect emotionally and report the facts, Amy.

Far be it for me to judge another person's "fantasy," but Jesus—it was a lot to take in once I stopped trying to block it out.

The genetic male perfection of a Krinar whose dick Ms. Emmy was riding was gently fingering her clit and worshipping her nipples, sucking on one perfect, pink areola at a time. But the things he was saying to her in between his nipple play belied the apparent sweetness of his touch. Because he was calling her a dirty slut. Telling her what a greedy whore she was being.

In contrast, the alien gripping her hips, controlling her positioning for his maximum penetration as he fucked her rear entrance, was groaning about how beautiful and precious she was, telling her what a good girl she was being for them and how sweet her tight asshole felt gripping his dick.

And still a third K was playfully taunting her as he fisted the roots of her hair and stroked his giant erection right in her face. "Show me how a good alien cumslut begs," he'd coax, before letting her lick the precum. He would allow her to wrap her bee-stung, begging lips around the fat head of his dick before yanking her by the hair off of him again and proceeding to stroke his cock just out of reach of her extended tongue until he was satisfied with her begging again.

My cheeks were so hot they hurt. My eyes burned from not blinking. This was so utterly twisted.

Positively horrific.

And horrifically hot.

I was so turned on I was sure Vair could feel it on his thigh through the thin fabric of my tags-still-on TJ Maxx dress. Definitely wouldn't be returning it for a refund now.

Focus on the facts. Just dictate the facts.

"Are you asking me for help with the facts?" Vair's chin settled on my shoulder.

Shit. I'd said that out loud?

"Feel free to interview me," he offered. His hard chest pressed along my spine, and the arm banded around my waist drew me deeper into his lap until my ass was nestled against his groin.

On the one hand, his proximity felt safe and comforting within the small room presently dominated by naked, huge, aroused male Ks wielding inhuman erections on the floating bed/stage in front of me. At the same time, the alien erection I felt hardening against the cleft of my ass was equally disruptive to what scant peace of mind I was clinging to. Then the palm of his other hand settled on my lower thigh just below the hem of my dress, and his finger began tracing lazy circles on my inner knee.

I couldn't get my brain and mouth to formulate a reply. Nor could I get my hands to stop shaking enough to make use of the electronic notepad he'd given me.

"Fact." Vair's low voice filled my ear as his lips brushed against it. "Human female has been enjoying extended orgasms at the hands, mouths, and cocks of multiple male Krinar for over thirty minutes now."

Was I supposed to jot that down?

I didn't. I was having difficulty just forcing enough air into my lungs.

"Fact: Female human has been injected with Krinar saliva at her own behest," Vair continued, "making her more receptive to orgasm, her body primed to engage in prolonged sexual intercourse with numerous partners."

K saliva—injected?

His slow circles were drifting higher up the inside of my leg.

"They didn't bite her?" I tried to sound analytical. Detached.

I totally failed.

"No. They did not."

Interview him like a reporter. You're a reporter. "Isn't the whole point of this club so Ks can drink human blood?"

"Yes. And no."

Helpful. "What—why a saliva injection?" I was panting now.

"Our saliva in your bloodstream is what induces the Ecstasy-like sensation and aphrodisiac effect that you so fondly wrote about in your article."

Was that a hint of bitterness I detected? Score one for Amy.

And this was valuable intel. *Focus on the intel.* "How? Why would your saliva—"

"Your blood contains the same hemoglobin characteristics as the Krinian primates who used to be our primary source of sustenance on our home planet before we hunted them into extinction millions of years ago."

Not the explanation I was prepared for.

His muscled thighs flexed and shifted beneath me, parting my legs as they did so. His hand drifted higher beneath my dress as if it had every right to, sending a thrill of anticipation straight to my lower belly—a thrill that contrasted sharply with the rush of fear that tripped my heartbeat.

"There's a chemical found in our saliva that was originally designed to make our prey feel drugged and docile, allowing us to feed from them without resistance."

This was fucked up with a capital F.

"That same chemical now has the effect of enhancing your human sexual experience when we bite you."

I was officially *prey*.

And I'd just spread my legs wider for the predator holding me.

"With the advent of synthetic hemoglobin substitutes and the manipulation of our own DNA over the past million years or so, we no longer require the blood of a sister species for survival."

Now they just did it for fun?

It was all so disturbing. Yet somehow hot… in a really wrong and dirty science-of-evolution kind of way.

"But w-why inject it?"

His hand was so close now. The heat coming off

of it between my thighs was sending my clit into a mad, fluttering frenzy.

"Because this way, the Krinar males remain in control of their own desires." His voice was patient as the tip of his knuckle made contact with my soaked underwear at long last—finding the evidence of my instinctive "prey" response. "They don't have to worry about getting carried away and fucking a human female too hard. Too fast. Humans are a fragile species. We've learned to be gentle with our food."

Cute. My E.T. had a sense of humor. *A sick one.*

"Makes it easier for them to focus solely on the human client's needs."

"Client?"

"Patron, subject, patient—whichever you prefer. We're also less territorial when we don't drink our prey's blood. Makes it easier to share."

Patient? Share?

I could feel my heartbeat in my sex as his knuckle began to lightly stroke me.

"How… that's not—this isn't sexy"—I gasped for air as he added more pressure—"at all."

Oh, God, who was I trying to convince? Myself? Vair? The three aliens waiting for their turn with the soap star who were now all watching me with hungry eyes as they stroked themselves, relishing the scent of my fear and arousal?

"Mmmm." Vair inhaled deeply against my neck. "I disagree, love."

"You aren't the food," I pointed out, directing a back-the-fuck-off glare at one of the Ks when he had the audacity to lick his lips while eyeballing me.

"Humans are obsessed with vampires." Vair's voice was amused. "They've romanticized them for centuries." His lips caressed my ear. "Fantasized about being their prey."

Damn, this was true. "Not all of us."

"Of course. Not *you*, Amy." He chuckled. "Never you. My turn to ask questions."

I didn't argue. I again was in Vair's world, playing by his rules, swiftly falling under his spell.

"Have you ever fantasized about being shared?"

I shook my head, relieved that it was an easy question.

He was still stroking me. Barely. *Lazily.* Just enough to keep me uncomfortably aroused and on edge.

"That's good. Because I'll never share you."

I was so hot I was melting.

"Tell me, are you enjoying the other male eyes on you right now?"

"No," I admitted breathlessly. "Not at all." Another easy one.

"Very good. I'm not enjoying it either."

He said something in his K language, and the air

shimmered and rippled in front of us as if it were water, before taking on a silvery, translucent quality that expanded the length of the room to form a wall between us and the other occupants—a wall that looked similar to a two-way mirror.

I hadn't a moment to ponder this crazy-impressive phenomenon, though, because Vair's finger hooked inside my underwear and tore the crotch clean out in one swift tug.

The cool air hit me where I was exposed and desperate to feel his hot fingers.

And so much more.

"Better?" he asked as he spread my legs wider with his knees and slipped his hand up over my breasts and around my neck.

I didn't answer. My heart hammered in my chest as his lips pressed to my ear and his fingers tightened around my throat.

"Fact: You're ready for me to fuck you now. So ready you're praying that I'll do it without you having to ask. You're hoping I'll bite you, aren't you? Give you the excuse you need to lose control and beg me to fuck you until you forget why you ever thought that playing it safe in life was a good idea.

"That's why you've been rocking back and forth, rubbing against my knuckle, grinding your perfect, luscious ass into my erection, isn't it? You've been hoping I'd lose control. Hoping I'd turn into a wild, savage predator who takes what he wants so you don't have to admit that you want it.

"Well," he continued with a dark chuckle, "you're in luck. I've been a very patient savage, Amy. For *a whole month.* I gave you time. Time to write your article. Time to sort things out in your mind. Time to come to me on your own terms. You didn't. Now it's happening on mine.

"I'm going to fuck you." He spoke the words slowly, his breath hot against my ear as my pulse beat frantically against his fingers. "Then I'm going to bite you." His voice was calm and even, belying the violent urgency radiating from him. "And then I'm *really* going to fuck you."

Immobilized by fear and excitement, I remained mute as his other hand pried the electronic notepad from my sweaty fingers. I didn't bother to notice what he did with it.

He removed my glasses next.

I didn't object.

"Take the dress off if you want to keep it."

I didn't move.

My body jerked reflexively as my dress and undergarments were shredded off of me seconds later.

CHAPTER TWENTY-TWO

Vair stood, unseating me from his lap. My naked body pitched forward, and I stumble-stepped, thrown off-balance in my high heels, until my palms found purchase against the strange glass wall separating us from the soap star's orgy.

I knew a moment of panic at being so completely exposed, standing there naked in my heels, my nose inches from the glass surface that felt solid and yet somehow alive—as fluid as water, moving and vibrating with energy beneath my palms—as I was afforded a front-row, up-close, and graphic view of the alien group sex session that was getting wilder by the minute.

No one on the other side of the glass was looking at me, though. I told myself they couldn't see me—that it had to be a two-way mirror given what Vair had said about not enjoying other male eyes on me. Still, I'd never felt more naked and vulnerable.

I took a step back, pushing off against the glass. But I didn't get far as my ass collided with Vair's hard thighs. His hands were suddenly everywhere, his body rubbing against and covering the length of mine from behind.

And my hands were… stuck.

Literally stuck.

That alien glass *was* alive. It had wrapped around and shackled my wrists to its surface. My hands were positioned at chest level, and I could see where the glass had morphed into thick, clear restraints around my slender wrists.

"Vair?" I sounded terrified.

I *was* terrified.

His right palm closed over mine atop the glass as his mouth brushed my cheek, whispering reassurances that failed to register as I continued to struggle in vain.

I immediately understood why people used safe words.

Because I needed one. And I didn't have one.

"Easy, darling." He linked his fingers with mine against the animated glass as his left hand fisted in my hair. "It's all right. The wall won't harm you." He tilted my head back. "I'd never let anything harm you."

"I don't like being restrained!" My eyes beseeched his—two dark pools of lust that studied me, and not without compassion, I noted, as he seemed to genuinely consider my plea. *Briefly.*

Then his lips brushed over mine in the first true, conscious kiss we'd shared since being reunited. "You'll like it this time," he promised softly. He nipped my bottom lip, tugged it gently between his teeth, and sucked. "Because you're with me." He leaned into me, his erection pressing unmistakably against my ass—so hard and huge it sent another wave of apprehension through me. "And you know I'll always keep you safe."

I didn't know that.

Why the hell would I know that?

His species was my planet's enemy. He was blackmailing me. He was restraining me against a moving, translucent wall straight out of a science fiction horror story, planning to fuck me while I was forced to watch the crazy erotic alien orgy taking place mere feet away on the other side of said creepy wall.

I'd never been so terrified and turned on in my life.

"I adore you, little human."

"Little human" was back to being an endearment, and he kissed me with none of the aggressiveness I'd anticipated when he'd first announced that he was going to fuck me, bite me, and then "really" fuck me—in that order. His gentleness took me by surprise as his lips caressed and nibbled until my own relaxed and allowed him to deepen the kiss.

"I worship you," he murmured before slipping his tongue inside my mouth in a languid, drugging kiss that made my whole body feel so heavy with need I was almost glad the wall restraints were there to hold me up. "Never harm you."

His words were nonsensical. Ks didn't worship humans. And he was sure to harm me.

My body didn't know the difference. Didn't care that he was the obvious threat that even my faulty instincts should've recognized.

I sagged into him, my nipples painfully erect and yearning for friction where the cool air was hitting them. Arousal flooded my sex and dripped down my inner thigh, my core clenching with the need to have him fill me. To push his alien cock in deep where it could never belong.

My body didn't care about the obvious facts of the matter—that this was completely dangerous and untenable territory. It wanted to lose control.

Because screw danger and consequence; sometimes a girl just needs to get fucked.

So I kissed him back the way a woman kisses a man when she wants exactly that, silently daring him to give it to me. Knowing Vair would deliver.

I swallowed his groan of approval as his hands skimmed over my goose-pimpled skin at last, his touch too light and brief against my trembling stomach and aching nipples to satisfy.

I spread my legs and tilted my ass into his groin in supplication.

He broke our kiss, his breathing labored as he said, "So sweet. Just like I knew you'd be."

His hand skated down my lower belly to touch between my drenched thighs before moving around to grip my butt cheek.

"This ass has haunted me for a month," he confessed, kissing his way down my spine until he was on his knees behind me, kissing, licking, and sucking the underside of my rear into his mouth in a way that was sure to leave marks.

As much as my ex-boyfriends had raved about my booty, none of them had ever given me a hickey there before. There was something so erotic, slightly taboo, and oddly humbling about the way Vair was worshipping my backside.

Hearing the noises that he was making and knowing how turned on he was just to be kissing my ass pushed me past the brink of my own long-held preconceived notions of decorum, well past caring that I was restrained by an animated glass wall and about to get eaten out from behind by a scary, dominant alien. I went up onto my toes in my heels, angling my ass higher for him as his fingers spread my fleshy cheeks apart to make way for his exploring tongue.

When that hot tongue made contact, licking the length of my slit from clit to anus, I lost it. And by "lost it," I mean I got loud.

As Vair proceeded to nibble, suck, and lick every millimeter of my exposed, over-stimulated privates, I threw years of well-ingrained, safe, proper behavior aside and started making noises that rivaled those coming out of the soap star on the opposite side of the glass—who was high on K saliva and getting fucked by a whole roomful of hot, hung Krinar aliens.

When all orgy eyes shifted in my direction, I realized that although they might not be able to see me, they were most definitely hearing me. And they liked what they were hearing. A lot.

I could tell by the way their irises glowed with excitement, the way their pupils dilated, and the way their movements accelerated—whether stroking their own cocks or moving inside the human client-slash-patron-slash-patient they were attending to—that the noises I was making turned them on immensely.

Their hungry eyes stared unseeingly in my direction, and I knew they were imagining the things that Vair might be doing to me behind the two-way glass partition.

I wanted to quiet down, but I couldn't.

It was all too fucking hot. So dirty and exhilarating I could scarcely believe it was happening.

And it was happening all right.

It was all too much to resist: the pressure of Vair's tongue moving against my clit, his fingers squeezing and holding my ass cheeks apart, his thumb stroking shallowly into my center.

And then his long, slickened finger began pressing inside me where no man had dared venture before, setting off a string of begging interspersed with profanity as I came apart against his face.

CHAPTER TWENTY-THREE

I had no time to get my bearings. My orgasm had barely receded and Vair was already standing behind me, his thick girth pressing steadily into my slick channel despite the residual contractions working against him.

My legs were shaking so badly they could no longer support my weight. The wall restraints and Vair were holding me upright—his big hands wrapped around my waist, his strong thighs pressed against the backs of mine as he drove his full length to the limit inside me.

A noise that was a cross between a grunt and a gratified scream escaped me when he bumped up against my cervix.

He felt bigger than I remembered. *Huge*, despite

how wet I was from my orgasm and the fluid still rushing to lubricate my sex for his entry.

But this was no mere entry.

It felt like primal possession—a deep and all-consuming invasion—as his fingers tightened around my waist to the point of discomfort.

A growl of contentment reverberated from his chest. I felt it resonate through me from the bottom of my toes to the tips of my imprisoned fingers. And I knew…

This was a claiming.

Any slim doubt I held of that fact was eradicated the moment he began to move. He plunged to the hilt with every thrust, his strokes controlled yet brutal—at once tender and ruthless in the way that he rammed deep, filling me to the point of distress even as gentle fingers continued to coax my slick bundle of nerves, his words of praise encouraging me to take more, to accept all of him.

He began spouting nonsense behind me, saying that I belonged to him, that I was made for him. Assuring me that I would mold to him—that my body was meant to accept his inside it for all eternity.

I knew that he was serious. Instinctively, I sensed that this was not standard K pillow talk or hyperbole he was engaging in when he promised that he was keeping me this time—that he intended to fuck me like this *forever*.

The realization of that fact wasn't something I could logically define. It was a deeper awareness—a visceral knowing. Something I felt in the thrust and drag of his cock as he filled places inside me no man had ever reached before. In the warmth that expanded within my chest as I sensed how much he wanted me—*needed me*—with him.

It was terrifying and wonderful.

Intoxicating and sobering.

But mostly, I was ill-prepared to process such complicated, dichotomous emotions while being restrained and getting plowed from behind as I watched an alien orgy in the basement of an x-club.

So I pushed it aside, chalked it up to my faulty intuition, disconnected and isolated it within the gray matter of my mind for further evaluation at a later time.

It was just sex.

Kinky, hot-as-fuck, earth-shattering blackmail sex.

There was no need to delve into unwelcome, confusing emotions, to try and discern the meaning of Vair's words or fathom any deeper intentions he held beyond fucking me into oblivion. Not when my whole body was taut with tension, my sex keyed up and primed for an explosion I was helpless to contain.

I was emitting primitive keening noises and panted grunts in time to the slapping sound of Vair's balls against my ass. Shouting things that were nonsensical. My pussy had never felt so used and so treasured.

And every single K in the divided room was getting off on the collective anticipation of my next orgasm. I'd somehow managed to upstage a gorgeous soap star for their attention.

They knew from the noises we were making just how well and good I was getting fucked on the opposite side of the mirror as Vair made up for lost time, and that knowledge was hotter than it should've been.

In general, the realization of how much I was enjoying this whole scene disturbed me greatly. *But not enough to stave off the swiftly approaching freight train of my orgasm.*

"That's it, darling. Let it out. Show me who you really are."

I shattered.

Violently.

Squeezing around the biggest cock I knew I'd ever have inside me, I felt the contractions deep within—stronger than I'd ever experienced. My inner muscles fluttered and squeezed and locked, wave after wave, milking and claiming Vair right back—demanding his capitulation.

Shackled to a scary, animated wall in the bowels of an alien sex club, bent over and getting fucked harder than I'd ever been in my life, I felt like anything but a victim as Vair's strokes became short and punishing, his breaths ragged, his Krinar curse words disjointed and loud.

I suddenly felt like *I* was the savage predator—the dominant, conquering species holding Vair and every other K in the room captive and at my mercy as my orgasm tore Vair's from him, sucking every drop of his essence from his powerful Krinar body and taking it deep within me… where I wanted it to belong.

CHAPTER TWENTY-FOUR

He collapsed into me.

Or maybe it was I who'd collapsed?

For a moment, I thought I'd blacked out, but then I realized the glass wall had simply gone dark—completely opaque. The sounds of the other Ks grunting and of flesh slapping on flesh had also been snuffed out, because my own labored breathing suddenly sounded overly loud in the too-quiet room that I shared only with Vair.

I could hear his breaths as well. Feel them fanning the top of my head.

The wall had released my wrists. I was sandwiched in between it and Vair, his arm around my waist holding me upright against him, his semi-hard cock still buried deep inside me.

His lips skated down the side of my sweat-dampened face, pressing kisses as he murmured, "Are you all right?"

I didn't have an answer.

I wasn't sure if I was all right.

I wasn't sure of what had just happened to me—if I would ever be all right again.

"I need you to be," he told me when I didn't respond. "Because we're not done, darling."

My muscles pulsed and tightened around him in reaction.

"That's my good girl," he purred in my ear. I felt him harden and lengthen within me in turn. "Always ready for me."

I winced as he withdrew; I was sore from our rough coupling. But more than that, it was the loss of him inside me that chafed. Even though it was only for a moment as he turned me in his arms so that I was facing him.

His hands gripped beneath my ass, and my heeled feet left the ground as he lifted my legs to wrap them around his waist. The wall felt cold against my damp back as he pressed me flush against it.

"I missed you," he said as his lips connected with mine. Tasting. Then *devouring.*

The tip of his hard cock prodded the tender folds between my thighs, and I clutched his shoulders, urging him closer, feeling my body melt into him as the gentle, erotic thrust of his tongue mimicked that of the thick organ working its way into me.

Arching my back against the wall for leverage, I angled my pelvis forward, rocking and grinding into him, encouraging his possession despite how sore and swollen I felt inside.

My need for him was stronger than the discomfort.

I felt crazy for wanting him so much. Crazier still at the prospect of this night coming to an end.

And it would have an end. It was virtually the only certainty that existed within this unsustainable dance we were engaging in.

Yet I wanted the moment to go on. Wanted these feelings and this connection between us to be real. To hold a place of permanency within me where I knew they had no right.

He thrust deeper, penetrating me to the hilt and making me gasp at the fullness. He stilled, letting me adjust.

Our foreheads met. His nose nuzzled mine as our breaths intermingled.

"Did you miss me?"

I wasn't sure what he was asking. Was he asking if I'd missed him since we'd seen each other earlier tonight? Or if I had missed him for the past month?

Either way, I didn't have an answer. Vair wasn't someone I could afford to miss.

"Do you remember this room from your last visit?"

I shook my head. I'd been in the basement of his x-club during my last visit? This was news to me. But not entirely unbelievable, considering that many details about the events that followed after he'd bitten me remained hazy in my otherwise-potent memories.

What stood out were the sensations I'd felt at his touch. The scent of his skin, the taste of his mouth and his sex, the sounds he'd made. I recalled, too, the many positions in which he'd taken me, but they were only snapshots of colorful imagery in my mind's eye, interspersed within the powerful waves of lust I'd ridden, over and over again.

I felt his smile against my lips. "Would you like to see *my* favorite memories?"

It was one of those Vair-speak questions that didn't require answering. He was going to show me, whatever it was.

I heard Vair's "memories" before I saw them as three-dimensional video images came to life all around us in the previously quiet space.

A nervous giggle bubbled up in my chest—more giddy than anxious—though there was nothing funny about the erotic images of us on display when I turned my head to take in this new footage from my first x-club visit.

To my surprise, I saw that I'd had sex with Vair while restrained before tonight.

And I had definitely liked it.

There was footage of Vair taking me from behind while I was bent over and tied to what looked like a padded sawhorse. Images of him fucking my upside-down mouth while I was bent backward, strapped to a bench.

My sex fluttered around him as I watched the shocking videos play out.

He began to move inside me. Slow and easy, but at an angle that was *so* deep.

My thighs flexed; my ankles tightened around his waist.

"You see how good we are together?" His teeth nibbled my earlobe. "How perfect?" His questions were delivered as statements of fact.

What I saw was that my E.T. was a kinky motherfucker—beyond anything my limited vanilla sexual experience had ever contemplated.

We were wholly incompatible.

In another hologram, I was restrained to one of those x-shaped Saint Andrew's crosses, moaning and screaming my head off as Vair knelt in front of me—his mouth and hands working my sex without mercy.

My insides clenched around Vair at the sight of it. I rotated my pelvis into him.

It might've been the hottest visual I'd ever seen. It was an image that I knew would stay with me. One that I couldn't—*didn't want to*—unsee.

We were clearly wrong for one another.

"You see why I had to have you back at my club?" His mouth was laving my throat now, his fingers tugging on my nipples.

I did see.

And yet I didn't.

"Are you all right, love?"

I nodded. Feeling overwhelmed. Needing more. Wanting less. Craving everything my scary alien lover had to give.

"Is this okay?" He dragged in and out.

Stretching me.

Soothing me.

Burning me up inside and making me ache for more.

I couldn't speak. I nodded again.

"I'm going to bite you, Amy."

It was a statement. But the way he announced it let me know that he would give me a choice in the matter—an opportunity to tell him no if I didn't want that.

It made me want it even more.

I nodded, tilting my throat up into his marauding mouth. My fingers slid through the silky hair at the back of his head, coaxing him closer as my hips ground and rotated against him, meeting his too-slow, too-gentle thrusts.

"Yes… that's it, darling. Show me. I'll give you everything you want."

His movements sped up, his hips thrusting and rolling between my thighs with renewed urgency as his mouth latched onto the column of my neck and his hand stole between our bodies to finger my throbbing clit.

I felt the sting of his bite and cried out, a sliver of fear racing through me as the slicing pain of his sharp teeth rent my fragile flesh. It hurt, burned in a perversely carnal way, and before long, the erotic, sucking pull of his lips and tongue wrenched an orgasm from me with a white-hot force that caused my vision to fade, my skin to burn, and my heart to race.

After that, I knew nothing but mindless pleasure, my body convulsing over and over through all-consuming climaxes, lost in a world where there was only Vair, only us, reaching for ecstasy that was nothing short of divine.

∽

I was vaguely aware of Vair bathing me at some point ages later—it might've been hours or days. Of Vair's coworker Shalee examining me afterward and taking my vitals in odd places and with foreign medical devices as she and Vair spoke in hushed tones.

I remembered being beyond wrecked, exhausted yet fighting the call of sleep, not wanting my night with Vair to be at an end. I remembered embarrassing myself by telling Vair so, saying that I didn't want to fall asleep and wake up alone inside my apartment again—like the first time I'd gone to his club. Then I tried to cover it up by complaining that it was his K saliva that had made me say it.

He kissed me and promised to be there when I woke up as he tucked me into the most comfortable bed I'd ever lain upon. I fell asleep shortly thereafter to the lulling sound of his deep voice speaking in Krinar, and to the sensation of his fingers combing lazily through my hair.

CHAPTER TWENTY-FIVE

My new sheets were rubbing against me in the most sensuous way. Lightly caressing and molding to my bare legs in a manner that was heavenly. My God, but they were soft. I would have to order another set of these—if I could remember when and where I'd gotten them.

Wait… had I gotten new sheets?

I noticed the room was too bright behind my closed eyes. My bedroom never got this much sunlight in the morning. Then I remembered that I'd been staying with Jay. Sleeping on his couch so that we could figure out what to do about me going to Vair's x-club the next—

Shit!

I jackknifed to a sitting position.

My heart racing, I gaped at my unfamiliar surroundings. I wasn't at Jay's. I was in a massive bedroom, with floor-to-ceiling windows along one wall revealing gorgeous views of clouds and sky. In a mad moment of sleep-deprived idiocy, I feared Vair had abducted me on his alien spaceship.

Then I jumped out of bed and saw the blessedly familiar skyscrapers of NYC below.

Below?

Jesus, I was high up. In a penthouse somewhere.

"Good morning."

At the sound of Vair's voice, I spun around so fast I nearly toppled over.

"Hi," I said automatically, my face flushed and my eyes wary as they met his. He was leaning casually against the wall by the door, and I realized that I must be in his bedroom.

Crap. I'd spent the night at Vair's place?

I glanced down and was relieved to note I wasn't naked. I was wearing a very soft, very *large* man's shirt. Vair's shirt, no doubt.

Vair was dressed for the day already, looking polished and elegant—and devastatingly attractive—as he stood staring at me with his dark, assessing gaze.

"Good morning," I said, sounding like an imbecile. I was out of sorts; I didn't know what to say or do.

He smiled. "The bathroom is that way if you need it." He pointed to my right. "You'll find towels and whatever toiletries you require."

"Great!" I practically shouted the word as I beelined in the direction he'd pointed, doing my best not to run, and also to mask my freak-out when I noticed that the bed and nightstands were floating above the floor in the same manner as the furniture in Vair's x-club basement room.

"Oh, and Amy," he called out just as I reached the open door to his lavish bathroom.

"Yeah?" I jumped and spun around, releasing a startled gasp when I found him standing directly behind me.

He caught me by the shoulders and steadied me on my feet, a frown marring his brow. He looked like he was about to ask me if I was all right in that way that he always did, so I headed him off.

"I *really* have to pee."

"Of course." He released my shoulders. "I only wanted to tell you that the bathroom, like the rest of the apartment, is intelligent. Equipped with Krinar technology that's programmed to respond to my voice, gestures, and mental commands. I haven't programmed it to respond to you yet, so you may need some help getting the shower settings the way you want them if you decide you'd like to shower this morning."

I'd stopped taking his words seriously after he'd referred to his penthouse as an "apartment." I'd shut down and disregarded them completely at the point when he'd implied he was going to program his shower to respond to my commands—like I'd be here using it so often that it'd be necessary.

I shook my head and waved him off with a shaky smile. "I'm just going to hit the head and be on my way, okay? I'll just… shower at home."

I shut myself inside the bathroom and locked it before he could get another word in. Then I forced in several calming breaths as I counted to ten.

Vair's bathroom was, in a word, ridiculous. My eyes feasted on black-and-white marble, an enormous sunken tub, and a walk-in shower sized for twenty people, with a wall of glass overlooking the city.

I couldn't deal. And I actually did have to pee.

There was no normal toilet, but there was an upright porcelain hollow cylinder with rounded edges where a toilet should've been. It was missing several critical toilet components, though—namely, water and a flushing mechanism.

Oh, what the hell. I sat on it and relieved my bladder anyway. I realized when I was done that there wasn't any toilet paper in the bathroom either. I cast my eyes to the ceiling. *Typical bachelor pad oversights apparently extended to aliens, too.*

I was contemplating my options when a warm breeze blasted my ass without warning. I leapt off the cylinder with a yelp.

Looking down into the white porcelain, I saw no trace of urine, even though there was still no water in the cylinder and there had been no flushing sound. I also felt clean and dry.

Well, it was different, but pretty darn handy, I had to admit.

The sink looked slightly more normal, but there were no controls or buttons on the faucets. Assuming it had motion sensors, I waved my hands under it. A soap-like substance came out, followed by water a few seconds later.

Huh. Neat.

After washing my face, I inspected it in the mirror, noting that I looked far better than I felt on the inside. My skin was clear and healthy-looking, and I didn't have terrible dark circles under my eyes, as I would've anticipated.

There was a brand-new toothbrush and a travel-sized toothpaste on the counter that I made use of. It'd looked as if they were there just for me, making me wonder what the Krinar did to clean their own teeth.

Despite all of the sweating I'd done the night before, I noted that I didn't stink. In fact, my hair and body felt freshly washed. Disjointed memories surfaced of Vair bathing me at some point during the night.

And of Shalee coming to check on me.

Even amid my waning bite-induced haze in the early morning hours, I remembered thinking that her methods for "checking my vitals," as she'd called it, were fairly unorthodox.

My pulse spiked as I recalled her inserting a slim medical device about the size of a tampon inside me. I plopped down onto a marble bench by the shower's entrance, hiked my feet up, and spread my knees wide.

After the amount of intense, rough sex I'd had with Vair—who was by any human standard, *huge*—it should've been painful merely to pee this morning. But I felt perfectly fine. And I looked perfectly fine down there—just like the first morning after I'd hooked up with Vair at his club. It had puzzled me that time as well, initially causing me to wonder if I'd only imagined the events of our first club encounter.

It was widely presumed that the Krinar had advanced healing technology, given what humans had been told of their extended lifespans. Was it possible that Vair and Shalee had utilized their Krinar medical technology on me? Just to heal my vajayjay faster?

As crazy as it was, it seemed like the best

explanation for how I'd managed to avoid soreness. But why would they do that? And without my consent?

Had they done other things to me?

Stripping off Vair's shirt, I stood and inspected the rest of my body in the wall mirror, noting that I had none of the marks or bruises that should've come with the way Vair had been holding and touching me the night before—squeezing and gripping my flesh like he couldn't get enough of it. There were no bite marks on my neck, either.

Nor on my ass.

As I scanned every inch of my person, it dawned on me how well I could view every detail, each tiny pore on my blemish-free skin.

My eyesight!

I wasn't wearing my blinder glasses. I had no idea where they'd even ended up after Vair had removed them along with my clothes.

Holy shit, had they done something to correct my lifelong vision impairment as well? Was that why I had been seeing better without glasses these past weeks?

But why would they do it? *Why me?*

I sat back down on the marble bench, rested my elbows on my knees, and dropped my forehead in my hands as Tauce's awful words about me being

Vair's property swam in my mind. *About how Ks take what they want and keep what they claim as theirs.*

Oh, God. It was no more than what Vair himself had said while ramming into me from behind in the x-club basement. He'd said that I belonged to him, that he was keeping me this time, and that he intended to fuck me for all eternity.

"Amy?"

I jumped at the sound of Vair's voice and his soft knock on the bathroom door.

"Are you finding everything you need in there?"

"Yes!" I called out. "Everything's fine. I—I'll be right out."

I slipped his shirt back on and exited the bathroom. He was standing outside waiting for me, his eyes soft, a subdued smile on his lips. It was almost as if he was *trying* to appear nonthreatening.

As if the predator that he was had scented my fear and panic.

He held his hand out to me. "Come. I'll show you around."

I slipped my hand in his and did my best to keep my cool as he led me through the grand opulence that was his "apartment."

The place was enormous. It had to have been the entire top three floors of the building.

Sleek and modern, elegant and minimalist, with floor-to-ceiling windows that stretched three stories high, the penthouse was a study in clean lines and architectural symmetry. And Vair's futuristic furnishings and technologically advanced appliances and equipment somehow complemented the more conventional marble surfaces and oak herringbone floors that were reminiscent of traditional Park Avenue residences.

As stunning as the space's interior was, the views from the windows were awe-rendering. We were no longer in the Meatpacking District—that much was certain. The view from the main room faced north, and we were high enough up that I could see clear across Central Park to the George Washington Bridge.

There were no words. But I found one.

"Wow," I breathed, my quiet morning voice lost in the grand space.

Much like me.

"Do you like it?" Vair's thumb stroked back and forth against the sensitive skin of my wrist.

I nodded. "It's… breathtaking."

It was a work of architectural genius. *On Park Avenue.* A coveted NYC residence that likely traded somewhere near the hundred-million-dollar range. And I was standing in it, looking out across Central Park—holding hands with the alien invader sex-club owner who lived in it.

I needed to leave.

He gave my hand a gentle squeeze. "Thank you."

At his words, I turned away from the view to find him smiling at me as if he was genuinely pleased by my reaction. "I'm glad you approve."

He didn't sound the least bit sarcastic.

I swallowed, fighting down the panicked voice inside me that was screaming, "*Run.*"

"You hardly need my approval," I said with an anxious laugh, feeling small as I stood there in Vair's oversized shirt—and gargantuan penthouse.

His hand shifted against mine, his fingers repositioning to link between my own.

"You don't need to be nervous, Amy." His thumb resumed its idle stroking.

My heart rate spiked. Blood pounded in my ears and my face prickled with heat. My stomach roiled and dark spots began to invade my vision. I suddenly felt more terrified standing there holding Vair's hand than I had been in the basement of his x-club, surrounded by aroused male Ks and restrained by an animated glass wall.

The fear was ludicrous—but also very real.

I knew Vair sensed it, too. Heard the concern in his voice that sounded so far away through the blood rushing in my ears as he asked me if I was all right.

Sheer will and the greater fear of embarrassing myself kept me from fainting on my feet as I closed my eyes and nodded.

"I'm afraid of heights," I mumbled, knowing that I had to tell him something. "I shouldn't have come so close to the window."

I was off my feet, cradled in his arms, and being carried across the room before I'd taken my next breath. He set me down on a white, floating couch-like surface and said that he'd be back. A moment later, he returned with a glass of light pink liquid, and I drank it all without even asking what it was.

That was the moment I knew the truth.

I was no longer afraid of Vair.

It wasn't the scary Krinar alien in him that I was panicking over.

It was the alien feelings and reactions he was inducing in me.

I needed to get it together and get the hell out of his penthouse.

I felt the weight of his warm palms on my knees as he knelt in front of me. I met his dark gaze—and immediately regretted it.

It wasn't the concern that I saw there that unsettled me, nor was it the sincerity. It was the understanding. The quiet knowing in his bottomless eyes that wordlessly projected that he totally got that I was full of shit. *And he was okay with it.*

"I know you're afraid of many things, Amy." His voice was low and gentle. "But I don't believe fear of heights is among them."

Neither of us dared to speak. You could've heard a pin drop. But it wasn't a pin that I heard; it was the theme song to *The X-Files* playing quietly in the distance.

My phone.

CHAPTER TWENTY-SIX

Jay had been messing with my ringtone settings while I'd been at his place yesterday. He'd reset my ringer to *The X-Files* theme song in an attempt to lighten the mood over my predicament with Vair.

My phone was ringing in my purse now. *Somewhere.*

"Ah… that's my purse," I said, setting my empty glass onto the floating coffee table next to me. "I mean, my phone in my purse. May I have it? I think I hear my phone ringing."

I'd had my phone inside my tiny evening bag when I'd gone to Vair's club. Tauce had stashed it in a hidden compartment within the upstairs bar last night, and I hadn't thought to bring it downstairs with me when we'd left for the basement.

"Of course." Vair stood with that catlike grace of

his, and left the room. My phone had stopped ringing by the time he returned and handed the purse to me.

My first shock in retrieving my phone from my bag was in seeing the time.

"Can it really be after eleven?" I protested, more to myself than to Vair. "I can't believe how late I overslept."

"You didn't fall asleep until almost four in the morning. You could use a few more hours of rest still."

"I'm fine. How much sleep did *you* get?" I countered defensively, sounding like an ornery child—and feeling like a scolded one. "You couldn't have gotten much more than I did."

"I slept three hours. Krinar don't require the same amount of sleep as humans."

They didn't? Oh. Well, that was convenient for them. Humans probably would've made more advances as a species too if we didn't need to sleep so much.

I stood and walked to the windows, tired of feeling Vair's eyes staring down at me. I needed space to think.

I began to pace back and forth as I flipped through my recent phone activity. There were two missed calls from Jay, twenty-nine from my parents, and eight new voicemail messages.

Fuck. It was Sunday. I'd told my parents I would call them, and I always called them before ten a.m. on Sundays. They'd probably called the NYPD, FBI, and National Guard by now. I'd long considered it a personal blessing that, barring evidence of violence or unusual circumstances, an individual had to be gone for twenty-four hours before they could legally be considered a missing person. Regardless of how many times my mother had been told this by law enforcement personnel, she persisted in trying to report me as a missing person whenever I failed to check in with her as scheduled.

There was a text from Jay saying to disregard his voicemail because he'd already spoken with Vair, which meant that the other seven voicemails were from my mom.

My eyes rolled. I couldn't decide whether it was over my mother's seven voicemails or the fact that Jay had been in touch with Vair while I'd been sleeping.

As I was concocting a plausible explanation—*lie*—for my parents, *The X-Files* theme song sounded again.

Shit. It was my mother. I didn't want to take it with Vair listening in, but I knew she would just keep calling and freaking out if I didn't. *And start calling everyone she knew in NYC to organize a search-and-rescue party.*

"Hey, Ma."

"Amy, is that you?" Her hysterical voice came through the connection at such high volume I jerked the phone from my ear.

"Yeah, Mom, who else would it be?"

"It's almost eleven-thirty," she shrieked. "Where have you been?"

"Oh, hey, sorry I missed your call. I, um… went to an early morning hot yoga class. It was great, but super-intense. And then I was so tired afterward that I crashed. I didn't even hear my phone ringing until I woke up just now."

I rationalized there was a partial truth in there. But I knew I sounded like a compulsive liar. I snuck a peek at Vair. His expression was stubbornly blank as he watched my pacing, his forefinger rubbing absently back and forth across his full bottom lip.

"Hot yoga?" My mom sounded confused on the other end of the line. Or horrified. I couldn't quite tell which as she repeated, "Hot yoga? You've been doing hot yoga?"

"Yeah, hot yoga. It's my new thing. Hey, so it's not a good time right now. I've got all these errands I'm behind on and that article I told you about that's due Tuesday. I'll call you guys later tonight, okay?"

"Amy, do you know how many people have died doing hot yoga? Didn't you read the articles I sent you about that Bikram guru who was sentenced to prison?"

Oh, geez. Why hadn't I fabricated a story about a community gardening project or something? I heard her yelling for my dad in the background and knew I couldn't do this right now.

"I've got to hang up now, Ma. I'll call you later." I disconnected the call and powered my phone off, then turned to face Vair.

"What?"

His expression was still annoyingly blank. "I didn't say anything."

"But you're judging."

"If you say so, love."

"You don't understand. You don't know my parents, okay? Sometimes it's better to tell a white lie with them." Why was I explaining myself? I didn't owe him an explanation.

He laughed. "On the contrary. I have a very good understanding of them. I must confess, your mother terrifies me."

"Ha! Right." The idea of Vair being terrified of my mom was comical.

"I mean it. Those emails she constantly sends you…" He shook his head, one brow arched high. "It's disturbing. Even for human behavior."

My breath caught. I felt like I'd been punched in the gut. He'd accessed my personal email account?

Jesus, why was I even surprised? The man—*alien*—had videotaped me without my knowledge or consent. I should've realized he'd have tapped into everything of mine that was personal and off-limits. Still... "You read my personal emails?"

"Of course, darling." Not a trace of contrition.

"I am not your darling. And my family's behavior is none of your business." How dare he judge my mom?

His smile slipped, his military-poster jaw tightening sternly. "I beg to differ. Everything about you is my business. Everyone who affects you is my business."

My stomach took another dive. He was one hundred percent serious.

"Rather high-handed, don't you think? Oh, right, you're a Krinar. Invading a lowly human's privacy is no big deal—totally within the realm of Krinar everyday behavior."

Protective and defensive instincts for my parents aside, his "even for human behavior" remark was gutting on another personal level, because it demonstrated just how low his view of my race was—and by extension, of *me*. Though, of course, how could someone who lacked the basic respect for my right to privacy view me as anything but inferior?

His eyes were thoughtful, yet his tone direct. "I only hope you understand that every time your parents say, 'Be careful,' they're saying, 'I love you.' You do know that, right?"

This conversation was not happening.

"Once again, Vair, what I do understand is that anything my parents say to me is my business and none of yours." I heard the echo of my words in the enormous room, and realized how much I'd raised my voice.

I needed to calm down.

"It's the only way they know how to express their affection for you—by constantly warning you of dangers and over-sharing their fears for your well-being."

I swallowed the unwelcome lump forming in my throat and forced a laugh. "Of course I know that. That's Psych 101 stuff. You should really stick to being superior at wall-dissolving and other K technology and leave emotional understanding to therapists."

He grinned, showing his perfect white teeth as he chuckled dryly. "Believe me, I wish I could at times. But there are many other Krinar with superior wall-dissolving skills and too few inclined to study human behaviorism."

I felt like I was missing an inside joke.

"Your parents programmed you to respond to fear. To constant threats of danger and intimidation. And you've grown up to be as terrified as you are fascinated by those threats." He shook his head and took a step in my direction. "You seek the truth above all else, and yet you lie most easily—especially to yourself. It makes you quite an interesting, delicious paradox, Amy."

He was fucking with me again.

Or maybe not?

He took another step closer. The space between us suddenly felt charged with sexual energy. I knew I had to dispel it.

"Fine." I tossed my hands in defeat. "You're right. I'm not afraid of heights. So I'm a bad liar? What the hell do you want from me?"

He didn't respond, so I filled the silence. "Look, I'm just an only child from Skaneateles with overprotective, paranoid parents. I probably should've taken the scholarship I was given and gone to college at Syracuse, close to home, like my parents wanted me to," I rambled as he stalked nearer. "But I wanted to get away on my own. So I spent too much on my college degree at NYU as a result. And now, at twenty-four years old, I'm just trying to make a go of it here in the city and work my way out of debt."

He kept moving fluidly closer. I retreated another step, then stopped myself.

"I'm not really even a very good reporter. Yet," I appended. "And when my boss kept giving me nothing but stupid fluff pieces, I got desperate."

He was close enough to touch me now. I knew I should stop all of my justifying and apologizing, but his soft black eyes encouraged me to continue.

"So I came to your x-club. I never meant to offend you or to upset the Krinar Council. I was just looking for an 'in'—a lucky break. A chance to write a real news story that would give the human public more helpful information about Ks than we've gotten in the two years since the invasion. Can't you try and understand that and stop punishing me for my article?"

His sigh fanned my forehead. "Amy, I already told you, I thought your exposé was brilliant. I have no desire to punish you for it, nor will I allow anyone else to."

"Then why are you doing this to me?" I blinked against the traitorous sting of tears. "Why are you blackmailing me?"

"I've already explained that as well, darling. You didn't come back to my club, and I needed you to."

"But *why?*"

"Because…" He smiled and brushed a stray wisp of hair from my forehead. "I'm an eight-hundred-and-forty-seven-year-old only child from Krina who came to Earth to try and help out with the transition and assimilation of our species. But after I saw you, I lost focus on all else. I found myself only interested in assimilating with you."

I heard the blood rushing in my ears again. I'd known that the Krinar were long-lived, but I'd never really contemplated it in quantifiable terms.

He was eight hundred and forty-seven years old?

And he wanted to assimilate with *me*?

Neither of us spoke as his fingers traced my jawline and stroked down the column of my throat, his feather-light touch sending a delightful thrill through me. So many questions swirled in my head. I posed the least significant one.

"You're an only child, too?"

He nodded, his mouth twitching at the corners. "Yes." He leaned into me, his lips ghosting over my brow. "As a result, I'm afraid I'm used to having my way, and I don't like to share." His tone, which had been light and playful, became stern and fervent as he said, "Which reminds me, I don't want you spending the night at Jay's anymore."

My back stiffened. I pulled away from him as my spine straightened. "I'm sorry… how is that your business? How do you even know—? Have you been spying on me?"

It was a dumb question. We both knew the answer was yes. We both knew he'd visited me the night before at Jay's. But it required asking nonetheless.

"Jay told me when he texted yesterday that you'd stayed with him Friday night."

Oh.

"But yes, actually, I have been spying on you," he continued matter-of-factly. "Quite intensely. It's my second-favorite pastime."

My stomach flipped at his admission. And the craziest part was that I wasn't sure if it was nausea or butterflies I felt.

I had been right. Vair had been keeping tabs on me everywhere.

And he didn't seem the least bit repentant about it.

CHAPTER TWENTY-SEVEN

"So... THERE *ARE* HIDDEN CAMERAS SET UP AT MY apartment, too? Just like at my office?" Another dumb question, but I needed to have it spelled out.

He stared me dead in the eyes as he answered without apology, "Yes. Several."

"Why?"

"I like watching you, Amy." His knuckles grazed my cheekbone. "A lot."

I swallowed. "In every room?"

"All the important ones."

What did that mean? "I don't understand."

But I did. I just didn't want to.

"It's simple, Amy." His lips dusted my forehead as I felt the weight of his words brand me in other places. "I like recording you. I enjoy watching you." He kissed my lids, my nose. "Especially when you touch yourself. In your bed. The shower. That one time in the living room…"

Oh, God.

"I like to imagine what you might be thinking. About me."

This wasn't hot.

"The naughty things you fantasize about us doing."

It wasn't hot.

My nipples disagreed. My pussy did too.

Everything about Vair that should not have been a turn-on to me somehow was. And there was nothing about it that I could rationally reconcile.

His arm locked around my waist, and his other hand slipped under my oversized shirt, between my ass cheeks, to cup my bare center from behind. I pressed both hands to his chest, pushing against him. He didn't move. "We have to stop," I protested. "We have nothing in common."

"You just said it yourself: We're both only children. As solid a foundation as any for a relationship."

I groaned. *This was all madness.*

"This can't work."

"My darling, it's already working." His mouth dropped to my neck, kissing and sucking the sensitive skin there. "You're dripping wet."

"But we're not… compatible." I moaned as his fingers found my drenched center.

My hands had found their way to his shoulders, but they were no longer pushing him away.

They were clawing him closer.

"I'm not a sex-club person," I tried to argue through the haze of lust swiftly enveloping me. "I'm not into all that… kinky… stuff."

I heard the quiet laughter deep in his chest, felt it in the quaking of his shoulders beneath my grip. "Of course you aren't, darling. Yet you endure it so well for me."

Before I knew it, I was being held high in his arms. We'd both been stripped naked by some force of K technology, and my legs were locked around Vair's waist. His hot tongue rhythmically stroked the depths of my mouth as the blunt tip of his erection pressed into my entrance.

And then he kept me there, his cock barely inside me, while he whispered filthy promises, his fingers teasing back and forth along the cleft of my ass to the point where we were joined—until I was desperately wiggling against his hold in my effort to shimmy down and impale myself.

Still, he didn't relent.

I took to begging when his fingers slipped between us and he proceeded to tease my clit until my insides clenched, my arousal dripping down to coat the stubborn, hard cock lodged too shallowly within.

But begging didn't satisfy.

No, only when I began to admit, at his prompting, to all the things that I liked about his club, to confess to my dirtiest masturbation fantasies, did he slowly lower me onto his thick shaft.

By that time, I was so thankful that I cried out with every inch given. I whimpered and arched my pelvis into him as he lifted and lowered me, going a little deeper each time, my body welcoming and worshipping his length as it stretched my walls and split me open until finally he was fully inside.

Then he seated us both in one of the floating chairs and told me to take what I wanted from him.

And I did.

With my legs astride his hips, my knees dug into the soft but firm surface beneath us, and I began to ride him, my hips circling, moving up and down, raising and lowering. He groaned as I sucked his tongue into my mouth, kissing him with a wanton abandon that matched my body's movements.

His fingers dug into my ass cheeks. His hips tilted up to deepen the penetration as I impaled myself over and over again. "So tight." He grunted. "So perfect."

His hands grew rough and urgent on my breasts

as I bounced and rolled my body up and down, lost in the sensation of his cock spearing me so deeply, relishing the freedom and control I had over our union.

His fingers pressed urgently against my clit, and I muffled my cries against his neck, my mouth latching on, sucking and savoring the scent and taste of his skin.

"That's it…" His voice was hoarse. "Just like that, darling. Mark me."

My inner muscles clenched harder at his words, gripping him possessively as I came undone.

"Fuck. You're all mine. *Forever*," he growled.

My internal walls seized around him and my teeth sank reflexively into his neck as my body flew apart, convulsing in orgasm.

He took control of our movements then, ramming his length into me, his big hands on my ass jerking me up and down in a rapid frenzy as he roared and cursed, emptying everything he had to give deep within me.

∽

After my mind-blowing orgasm had receded and my brain was able to process things beyond blind lust, I settled into a bout of post-coitus remorse once more. Vair's "all mine forever" proclamation may have had something to do with it—reminding me of Zyrnase and Tauce's remarks about me being "Vair's human."

Krinar property.

I remained quiet as Vair and I showered together. After our shower, he insisted on shining a strange red light from a thin silvery medical device over any areas where he feared he'd left bruises or scratches on my skin. He explained that it utilized nanocyte healing technology.

I allowed it. But when he wanted to insert the tampon-sized healing device Shalee had used on me in order to heal any potential internal abrasions, I snapped and more or less told him to chill his shit, saying that my pussy and I weren't that fragile and that I didn't mind having an ache to remember him by for the next few days.

I probably should've left it at that when he backed off and didn't press the issue, but instead, I brought up the mystery of my improved eyesight, and asked him point-blank whether he had done something to heal my vision.

His answer was an unapologetic yes, confirming what I had already pretty much known.

Once again, I fell silent, conflicted over whether to be grateful or angry about his interference.

I watched with detached fascination as he fabricated clothing for me to wear out of thin air—a long-sleeved, lightweight casual tunic dress in a pale shade of blue, along with a pair of nude low-heeled shoes. This explained his ability to make those rapid wardrobe changes I'd witnessed. Or more accurately, his ability to get naked in seconds flat.

It was all very surreal. So foreign and overwhelming that I felt myself detaching more and more to avoid freaking out. Because in the back of my mind, I was growing increasingly afraid that he wouldn't allow me to leave.

"So... what happens next?" I finally worked up the courage to ask as I slipped on the shoes he'd made me.

"Well, I was thinking we might eat a very late breakfast together," he proposed with an adoring smile. "Maybe go for a stroll. Talk. We could also stay here," he offered, a hint of something carnal in his dark eyes. *The alien was insatiable.* "What would you like to happen next, Amy?"

His indulgent smile and the gentle way he'd asked that almost made me want to go for that stroll with him.

But I had to know where I stood.

I swallowed. "Um... I'd like to go home. To my apartment. Alone?"

He stared at me for a beat, pursed his lips, and nodded slowly. "Okay. Zyrnase can take you. Or

Robert. But I'd like for you to eat something before you go if you're up for it."

He was going to let me go? Just like that?

And there was a Krinar named Bob?

"And then I can go? If—if I eat first?"

His dark eyes turned stony. "Amy, you can go now, without eating, if you like. But I think you'll feel better if you get some food into your stomach. We had a long night together. And morning."

He was really letting me go?

"But what you said before about, um… me belonging to—I mean, being *all yours*—"

"You're not my prisoner, Amy." His voice was flat, his tone weary. "I'll get Robert for you." He left the bedroom.

And he didn't come back. Not even to say goodbye.

Eventually, Zyrnase came to tell me that my ride was downstairs.

The Krinar named Bob wasn't actually a Krinar at all. He was a middle-aged human guy from Queens. He drove me back to my apartment.

Alone.

CHAPTER TWENTY-EIGHT

AFTER BOB DROPPED ME OFF, I WENT TO JAY'S PLACE to grab the stuff I'd left there the night before. I ended up listening to him rave about Shalee, Vair's gorgeous and brilliant Krinar medical associate, for hours.

Jay was utterly smitten with her, even though he continued to profess that it wasn't serious, that they were only planning on having some fun together.

"You know, it's just that she's bi and I'm bi, and we're both into science and medicine and all—"

"You're into science? Since when? And *medicine?* Jay, having a lot of prescriptions in your bathroom cabinet doesn't count."

"Whoa!" He laughed and made an angry cat noise, throwing the claw gesture my way. "Someone didn't get bitten hard enough at the club last night."

He rambled on about Shalee some more, then offered to let me crash at his place again, but I declined. Not because I feared Vair's disapproval, but because I needed to be alone for a while.

Exhausted, I made my way home, and after calling my parents back and listening to my mom lecture me on the dangers of hot yoga for over forty minutes, I climbed into bed early.

And then I stared at the ceiling, wide-awake for most of the night.

∼

I GOT THROUGH MONDAY IN A CONSTANT STATE OF exhausted panic, expecting Vair to show up any minute and demand that I get into his limo and go back to his club. I imagined Tauce's angry yellow eyes following me around every corner, heard his nasty voice in my head, sneering that I was Vair's "property."

I couldn't eat. I didn't sleep well the next night. And I couldn't write.

When Tuesday came and I'd failed to finish my article about the Ks' forced vegan diet, I turned in the article I'd written weeks ago on the conjoined puppy twins—a month after my editor, Gable, had wanted it, and after every other news source in the city had already covered it.

I was probably going to get fired.

Meanwhile, Jay surprised everyone at *The Herald* by turning in a well-written opinion piece on the similarities between Krinar and humans, highlighting universal traits of emotional intelligence that both species shared. He even worked in anecdotal evidence of Krinar "butthurt" behavior, changing names and descriptions of key Krinar, of course, in order to "protect the innocent"—*and his ass*. Jay's K article was probably the only thing that saved *my* ass for the week with our boss.

By Wednesday, I'd started panicking that Vair *wouldn't* show up demanding that I get into his limo. By Thursday, the fear that I'd never see him again had crept in.

But then he texted me that evening. He sent a video. *Of us*. With a message to watch it and to think of him… because he was thinking of me.

I didn't text back.

But I watched the video. And I ended up fingering myself on my living room couch. Knowing that Vair was watching. And likely recording it.

I'd reached the pinnacle of dysfunction.

By Friday, my stomach was in knots as I anxiously awaited Vair's next move—quietly hoping that he would call or text, and, ideally, blackmail me into going back to his club that weekend.

I made a mental note to call my therapist and see if she would still see me on a sliding scale.

A little after three in the afternoon on Friday, Jay poked his head into my office and told me to grab my purse and meet him by the rear stairwell in ten. Thirteen minutes later, we were meeting with Jay's college friend and CIA agent in a little rundown coffee shop located on the fringe of the Financial District.

"Great to see you, man," Jay told him with a grin before turning to me. "Amy, this is Stephen, my friend from college that I told you about. Stephen, this is Amy."

We shook hands, grabbed coffees, and found seats at a quiet corner table. Jay's CIA friend, Stephen, was a tall, blond-haired, blue-eyed all-American type who looked like he should be in NYC hitting casting calls rather than working for the CIA National Clandestine Service. But then he started talking, and I totally got it.

"As I'm sure you know, Ms. Myers, two years ago, after the Great Panic, our world governments entered into the Coexistence Treaty with the Krinar, allowing them to establish settlements across the globe. We've since done our best to cooperate with the Krinar Council in order to coexist with these Ks. For the most part, they chose warm climates and isolated, sparsely populated areas to construct their main K Centers." Stephen paused his slow, monotone delivery to take a sip of his black coffee, and I slipped Jay my most discreet side-eye.

"They built settlements in Costa Rica, Thailand, and the Philippines. But there are also some K Centers here in the U.S. There's one in New Mexico, Arizona—"

"Stephen, man," Jay interrupted. "This is intel that we can get on Wikipedia or a general Google search. Can you tell us why Amy is on a government list?"

Thank God.

"Right. I was just getting to that. As you well know, while many humans despise the Ks and remain fearful and resentful of their sovereignty, there are those who view them as gods, and worship them as such." His speech and posture mimicked that of an unhip fifty-year-old. It was hard to believe he was our age. "Xeno-clubs, or x-clubs, sprang up almost immediately outside of the K Centers as places for Ks and K-worshipping humans to… interact." He made air quotes at "interact," prompting unwelcome flashbacks to the four-hour conversation in which my mother used nothing but euphemisms to explain the act of sex to me.

Then he paused, turning his attention fully to me. "Ms. Myers, I understand that you are familiar with these x-clubs. Is that correct?"

"Stephen, you know she is. She's the Amy Myers

who wrote *The Herald* article on the x-club located here in New York City. Can you please speed it up? We have to get back to the office sometime tonight."

"Of course. Of course. In the past two years, there have been more and more troubling cases of Krinar and humans *overindulging* in these x-club… interactions."

He made air quotes again at "interactions," and I nearly got up and left. I settled for furtively checking my phone for new text messages from Vair.

Damn it. Still nothing.

I blew on my coffee and took a sip.

"At first there was concern over the addiction aspect and the potential long-range effects of these K interactions. But then there were fatalities."

The coffee I'd just swallowed turned sour in my stomach. "I'm sorry—*what?*"

"Fatalities?" Jay shot me a nervous look. "You mean… from K bites? Humans have died? At x-clubs?"

"K *addicts* have died," Stephen stressed. "Xenophiles."

I couldn't help but notice he'd said it in a way that made it seem as if he felt they deserved it.

"How?" Jay asked, his face paling as he absently palmed the side of his throat. "From blood loss?"

"We aren't certain."

"From withdrawal?" I had to ask it. My cheeks reddened as Stephen shot me a scandalized look.

"We don't know." To his credit, his monotone didn't falter. "The Krinar Council gave our government very little information. But they assured us that the Krinar researcher they were sending here would investigate the matter thoroughly and implement strict controls for all x-clubs going forward. Our government agreed to provide whatever support was needed for the K researcher and his team to establish an underground x-club here in the city, and to prevent human interference with the organic selection process necessary for their study. The idea being that New York City's dense, diverse population provided access to a broader human gene pool for Vair to analyze than the rural, remote areas around the K Centers where these fatalities had occurred."

"Vair?" In my shock, I think I whispered it. At the same time, Jay had nearly shouted it.

"Yes, that's the name of the head Krinar researcher the Council sent." Stephen turned to me. "I believe you know him, Ms. Myers." His tone and expression didn't alter, but I knew I saw judgment in those blue eyes. "From what we understand, he's a behavioral scientist. Isn't that correct?"

My lungs felt compressed. I shook my head and

struggled to breathe as I stuttered, "I—I don't know… anything… about him. Behavioral—?"

"We aren't certain of his exact title or position within Krinar society," Stephen explained, "but we've been led to believe that he is more or less the Krinar version of an esteemed psychologist or behaviorist."

"Wait a minute," Jay interjected. "You're telling us that Vair is a sex therapist on Krina?"

"No. I'm telling you he's the head researcher that the Krinar Council sent to collect empirical data on the short- and long-term effects of blood and saliva sharing between Ks and humans."

"Empirical data?" Jay intoned with disbelief. "From a sex club?"

Stephen paused to take an annoyingly long sip of coffee before answering. "Yes. Testing the side effects of Krinar saliva on humans. Recording withdrawal symptoms, measuring how quickly humans become addicted. Also measuring how quickly Ks become addicted, researching potential cures—that sort of thing."

Oh, my God. I was a guinea pig?

An alien sex-lab rat?

Pieces began to fall together in my mind, forming a most disturbing puzzle. I recalled Vair's offhand remark on Sunday about too few Ks being inclined to study human behaviorism, and the way that he'd referred to his human clubgoers as *subjects* and *patients.*

"So what's the government list that Amy is on?" Jay asked, bringing me back to the point of this meeting.

"It's called the *charl* list," Stephen answered.

"Charl?" Jay's eyes lit up. "Amy, remember when Zyrnase and Tauce—"

"What does it mean?" I cut in.

"Charl are a class of humans under Krinar protection. Our government no longer has any jurisdiction over them. Actually, neither does the Krinar Council, it would seem, without the express permission of the Krinar whom the charl belongs to."

"Belongs to?" Jay gaped at his college friend. "Excuse me?"

"Our division intended to squash Amy's article, fearing that it would interfere with Vair's testing—give the whole x-club research program away. It's unusual enough having an x-club here in the city, so far from a K Center. According to my sources, the Council was in agreement and didn't appreciate her article drawing attention to Vair's testing facility either. But Vair stepped in and claimed Amy as his charl, forbidding both the Council and our government from doing anything to obstruct the circulation of her x-club exposé."

Vair had let my article run? He had opposed the U.S. government *and* the Krinar Council in this? More importantly, he'd *claimed* me as belonging to him and gotten my name on some government "off-limits" list?

"How many humans are on this charl list?" Jay asked.

"I'm not at liberty to divulge those statistics."

"How can a K just claim a human being?" Jay objected. "And how the hell can our government go along with that?"

I loved Jay for asking it, but I feared the answer was obvious: Ks were above our human laws. Our government had to go along with whatever they wanted.

"We don't have a choice," Stephen confirmed. "As I've said, we do our best to cooperate with the Krinar Council in order to coexist with the Ks." Stephen's eyes swept the largely empty coffee shop before he added, "A division of Homeland Security here in the city got into a heap of trouble shortly after K-Day for interfering with one of their charl."

He'd glanced disapprovingly at me when he'd said the last part.

Jay took notice. "She's not one of their *charl*, Stephen. She's a human being, a U.S. citizen, and a damn fine journalist. What can you do to help her?"

Stephen shook his head. "I've just told you, I can't do anything."

"What about the FBI? Or hell, I don't know, the United Nations? Anyone? Come on, there has to be some covert anti-K organization out there that will help us, right? A charl safe house somewhere?"

"No. There's nothing. And it wouldn't help anyway. The Ks have ways of tracking their charl. There's nowhere anyone would be able to hide her."

"You've got to be kidding me! You called me back and asked to meet with Amy just to tell her she's fucked? That she's registered as K property and there's nothing our government or any world organization can do about it?"

"No, I requested to meet with Amy because I wanted to ask her to stop writing x-club articles." Stephen's eyes shifted to me. "Regardless of Vair's decision to indulge you as his charl, your article *has* interfered. Whether you meant it to or not, your exposé popularized Vair's x-club, bringing it to the attention of innocent, naïve humans who otherwise wouldn't have known about it or gone looking for it. If you care about your country and your own race, you'll cease drawing attention to the 'Ecstasy-like' high attained from the sharing of blood and saliva between Ks and humans. You won't risk glamorizing what we know to be a dangerous and potentially fatal addiction to these aliens."

CHAPTER TWENTY-NINE

Jay fretted, ranted, and apologized at a mile a minute throughout the short cab ride back to our office. I barely heard him as I stared unseeingly out the window.

Once back at *The Herald*, I went through the motions of pretending to be working for the rest of the day.

I snapped out of my scared, confused, comatose stupor at 5:30 p.m., when I received the long-awaited but now-unwelcome text message from Vair inviting me to come back to his club that night. I texted back that I wasn't his property, stating in all caps that I would never in this fucking lifetime be his charl.

He didn't respond.

I waited ten minutes before shooting off another

angry text telling him that I wasn't interested in being bitten and fucked to death as his sex-lab rat either.

No reply.

I wanted to call him out as a fraud and a liar, but it occurred to me that Vair had been telling me the truth for the most part—in *Vair-speak*—all along. And that only made me more upset.

So I sent another text saying that if he ever came within three hundred feet of me again, I'd appeal this bogus charl business at the highest level within the Krinar Council—even though rationally, I knew they wouldn't give a damn about my rights or about helping me.

I didn't hear from Vair all weekend.

I continued to send him angry texts. I barely slept, and I neurotically checked my phone for a reply from him.

At night, I lay awake in my bed, contemplating what satisfaction I might get out of charging back to his club and screaming at Vair to go to Krinar hell in person. But those fantasies somehow always took a wrong turn as they played out in my mind's eye, often culminating with me shackled to an animated glass wall or a Saint Andrew's cross, and screaming at Vair for other reasons entirely.

So I didn't go back to Vair's club that first weekend.

But Jay did. He went to see Shalee.

He said he intended to question her about the xenophile fatalities Stephen had told us about. But beyond that, he said that he wanted to understand how Krinar saliva worked in the human system as an aphrodisiac-slash-narcotic in order to determine, as he put it, if the most profoundly intense sexual experience of his life was about Shalee or just her spit.

When he stopped by my office on Monday morning to catch me up on how his visit to the club had gone, our editor and boss, Richard Gable, was just leaving, having delivered a rare "job well done" on the article I'd turned in that morning about the potential future perils of the Ks' forced vegan diet.

"Top shelf, Myers! I really do miss my bacon." He clapped Jay on the shoulder as they passed each other. "Afternoon, Jay."

Jay gave him a fake bright smile and returned, "Afternoon, Dick," just like he always did. And like every other time, Gable reminded him that Dick was his father's name, and that he went by Gable or Richard.

It was the most juvenile, stupid gag, but something in Jay's delivery each time kept it from getting old. I shook my head and smothered the smile breaking out on my face until we were alone and Jay had closed my office door.

He had texted me on Sunday night to check in and let me know that he was okay, saying that he was too tired to talk but would fill me in at work the next day. Judging by the satisfied, relaxed expression on his face and the bounce in his step, it seemed that he'd had a good visit to Vair's club.

I pushed thoughts of Vair and my own hurt feelings aside and asked, "So? How'd it go with Shalee?"

"Great. And before you ask, *Mom*, the answer is no, she didn't bite me again."

That was a relief. I had made Jay promise not to indulge in another K bite after what we'd learned from Stephen.

"But we did do other things." Jay's grin widened, and the most adorable flush crept up from his neck to his cheeks. "And I think… I think maybe the chemistry we have is about more than just spit."

After gushing about Shalee for ten minutes, he went on to relay what she'd told him about the fatalities that had happened at the x-clubs near K Centers. Shalee had explained that because so few Krinar and human pairings existed on Krina, little was known at the time of the invasion about how often or how much Ks and humans should indulge in blood and saliva sharing. And unfortunately, not enough research had been done since, prior to Vair's team arriving in NYC.

She'd told Jay that in the case of a love pairing between a Krinar and a human, the Krinar's concern for the charl's human frailty would naturally prevent them from overindulging. But in the case of these more casual x-club encounters, there was often less thought given to safety, because actions were driven by pure lust and judgment clouded by bite-induced delirium.

Also, the humans going to these clubs would sometimes hook up with multiple Ks per night, thus having too much blood taken, too frequently. This explained the need for an x-club enforcer like Tauce —a K terrifying enough to hopefully scare the most overindulging xenos from coming back, in order to save them from themselves.

Shalee had then said that the answer was more research and stricter regulations moving forward, confirming what Stephen had told us.

"Listen, baby girl, I know you're upset and you feel betrayed. And believe me, I was ready to punch Vair out over that archaic charl alien ownership shit when Stephen told us about it on Friday. But after talking to Shalee, I think maybe being on the charl list isn't as bad as it seems."

"Jay, he claimed me as his *property*."

"Yeah, to protect you from both his government and ours, *and* to let you have your journalism success, which you never would've had otherwise since both the Council and our government were planning to put the kibosh on your x-club piece."

"Are you listening to yourself? Like I give a damn about journalism success if it comes at the price of my freedom as a human being."

He rolled his eyes. "Right. But Amy, look around you. You're sitting in your office, you just wrote another K article for *The Herald*, and you're going to go home to your apartment tonight just like you've done for the past seven nights, not to mention the past month, with no interference and virtually no contact from Vair—other than the one time he made you go to his x-club."

These were all valid points that should've made me feel better. But for some reason, I felt even more deflated.

"He fixed my eyesight without even asking me."

"Oh, what a villain." Jay raised one brow at me. "Face it, you're not exactly being treated like a prisoner. Come to think of it…" He winced and sucked air through his teeth. "The guy left you alone for *a month*, even after he'd claimed you as his charl. *Yikes.*" He shook his head, giving me a phony pitying look. "If anything, maybe you should be concerned that he only did it to be nice and he's just not that into you."

I wasted no time calling Jay out for his obvious K-sympathizer matchmaking attempts as he succumbed to a fit of laughter. I told him I was happy for him about Shalee, but that he needed to get his lovesick ass out of my office before I pulled the big three-prong hole puncher on him.

And luckily for him, he did.

CHAPTER THIRTY

I WAS LESS ANGRY ABOUT EVERYTHING AFTER MY CHAT with Jay on Monday. By Wednesday, when I still hadn't heard from Vair, I realized that I was depressed.

By Friday night, with still no word from Vair and with Jay's time monopolized by Shalee, I realized that I was lonely—although it took drinking two glasses of red wine alone in my apartment to admit it to myself.

In my tipsy state, I thought about changing out of my ugly pajamas and catching a cab to Vair's club. But I put the wine bottle away and got out the chocolate ice cream instead. I spent the rest of the night composing and deleting numerous text messages to Vair.

Saturday came and went with still no contact.

And Sunday marked two weeks since I had last seen Vair.

At that point, I began to fear that he might again go a month without seeing me. I even started to question whether Jay's teasing comment had been right and that perhaps Vair just wasn't that into me.

But then I reminded myself that he *could* see me… if he was watching.

So I decided to give him something to watch. After all, I'd gotten a text message from him inviting me back to his club after the last time I'd fingered myself in the living room.

I started with a little masturbation show in the kitchen to warm up—unsure if that constituted an "important room" where Vair would've set up surveillance. Embolded by how empowered I felt afterward, I donned a new bra and panty set and pleasured myself in the bedroom.

The next morning, I was ecstatic to wake up to a text message from Vair: another video of us. Upon watching it, I was inspired to give a performance in the living room on top of the coffee table—dressed for work in my most prim blouse and pencil skirt.

By lunchtime on Monday, I was so aroused that I considered locking my door and giving Vair another show right there in my office. Fortunately, sanity prevailed and I went to grab a coffee and a salad at the deli downstairs instead.

It was close to quitting time and my fingers were flying over the keyboard when a tall, dark, sexy-as-hell Krinar strode into my office as if he owned *The Herald.*

He'd already shut my office door and was leaning casually against it as I struggled to breathe normally, wondering whether I'd gone totally mad and was simply imagining him there.

Dazed, I stood and walked out from behind my desk as I stared at him in disbelief.

"I missed you, Amy."

He looked huge standing in my tiny office, nearly blocking out the entire door as he took me in with those intense, all-consuming black-brown eyes.

"Did you miss me?"

My nipples responded before I found the voice to do so. My inner muscles followed suit.

"I—I'm at work, Vair." I said it as much for my own benefit as his.

He smiled. "I know. And I need to watch you take what you want. Now. While at your work." His eyes darkened along with his tone. "Bend over your desk for me."

A shiver coursed through me. And Lord help me, but I didn't hesitate for a second. I just turned around and did it, flattening my hands against the cool, hard laminate desktop as Vair jerked my pencil skirt up around my waist.

I couldn't think. I was already panting, my whole body hot as my sex came alive with need.

"Spread your legs, darling."

I did.

He made a noise of approval as his hand moved down over my bare ass to rub against the damp thong between my thighs.

"All the way." His other hand pressed gently against the small of my back, flattening me to the desk as he tugged my thong to the side and worked two fingers into me to the knuckles. I was so slippery wet they met no resistance.

Fuck, I had missed him.

"Very nice," he praised, sliding his fingers in and out, rotating and scissoring them.

With my cheek pressed to the cold surface of my desk, my half-lidded eyes faced the door to my office —*that wasn't locked.*

I felt an increased heat behind me and knew that he'd silently shed his clothes in that magical way he'd done before.

This was happening. He was going to fuck me in my office at *The New York Herald*.

And I was going to let him.

None of this was sane. None of it was safe.

Safety had long become overrated.

He removed his fingers, and I felt the smooth, blunt tip of his cock prodding against me where I was more than ready to accept him. I tilted my hips back, encouraging his entry.

"That's it, angel. You do it. I want to see you take me deep inside."

I gripped the sides of my desk and rocked back into him until the broad head of his cock slowly pushed inside.

"So perfect." He exhaled, and it was the most carnal sigh I'd ever heard. "Look at you stretching around me."

I bit my lip and stifled a moan as his fingers stole around the fabric of my bunched-up skirt to stroke between my split folds where we were joined.

"So slick for me." His thumb circled my clit. "Take all of me, darling."

This was crazy.

I'd gone completely mad.

I envisioned Vair staring down at my spread privates in the glaring daylight streaming through my office window. Watching me as I slowly impaled myself on his huge alien erection.

During office hours.

With my door unlocked.

I needed to get my head examined.

"More, love." His thumb pressed and rolled, toying with my swollen, throbbing flesh. "It's all for you."

I let out a soft grunt as I slid all the way back,

stretching around the thickest part of his cock until I felt his balls pressed up against my wet center.

He groaned. "Such a good little human."

His patronizing endearment shouldn't have warmed my heart so much. Nor should it have made me clench and gush anew around him.

I was a goner.

A shameless K addict where Vair was concerned.

"Move on me."

It was an order.

I obeyed without question.

Going up onto my toes, then back down on my heels, I rocked back and forth on him. His fingers stroked and pinched my clit. His other hand caressed the backs of my thighs and ass.

"That's it. Faster, darling. Let me see you take what you want. Don't be afraid."

White-knuckling the sides of my desk, I let my body go, undulating back and forth, delighting in every rigid inch of him as his heavy cock dragged in and out of me.

I was already sweating. My cheap office desk had begun to make creaking noises under the strain of my movements. My computer screens were teetering and rattling atop the desk.

Still, I sped up at his command.

Knowing someone might hear. That we could get caught.

Because I couldn't stop.

"Harder." His fingers dug into the flesh of my ass cheek. *"Deeper.* I want to feel you come all over my cock." His voice was sounding less controlled. More urgent.

Then he began making a low, sustained growling sound deep in his chest. His fingers grew less gentle on my clit. His big palm mauled my ass in a bruising grip.

I knew he was restraining himself—eschewing his predator instinct to drive into me fast and hard for the sake of watching me take what I wanted.

And that just made me all the hotter for him as I sawed back and forth, my eager body swallowing every hard, thick inch.

"Fuck me like you'll never get enough, Amy," he snarled.

Something in my psyche broke at the harsh truth of those words, and I cried out as I suddenly flew apart, my movements graceless and jerky, my climax overtaking me.

His hand clamped over my mouth, and he drove his hips into me. His cock seemed to have swelled impossibly larger, and his strokes were rough and deep as my inner walls fluttered and squeezed around him, riding out the final waves of my ecstasy.

My legs were trembling from exertion, and my entire body felt like a wrung-out ragdoll as he pulled out and maneuvered me to my knees in front of him. His cock pushed past my panting lips into the back of my throat without preamble, and he spilled his hot seed as I gagged and swallowed reflexively around him.

His Krinar essence coated my throat and settled in my stomach, bringing with it the stark realization of what I'd just done and where.

But before complete and utter post-coitus remorse could set in, Vair groaned in pleasure and spoke the only words capable of eclipsing the horror of all else in that moment.

"*Fuck.* I love you, little human."

I had a history of having awkward, bad reactions to those three words. And it had never once in my wildest imaginings occurred to me that I might hear them from Vair—a *Krinar*, a member of the ruling enemy alien species.

I was in a state of shock as Vair withdrew from my mouth, picked me up off the floor, and proceeded to gently straighten my clothing and hair for me.

He then sat me down atop the edge of my desk.

"Are you all right?"

I didn't respond, my mind too busy shutting out his revelation.

He captured my face between his hands and tipped it up to his. "Amy, I had your office soundproofed weeks ago. Zyrnase is standing watch outside your door. It's okay. No one saw or heard us."

I suppressed a nervous giggle at his revelation. It was both comforting and disturbing to know he'd taken the precaution—*and liberty*—of soundproofing my office.

And why not? He'd already taken the liberty of bugging it with all manner of high-tech surveillance equipment.

I shook my head. Swallowed. "We can't… we can't do this. Anymore."

The soft concern that had been in his eyes morphed into something a shade colder. Darker. "And why is that?"

I pulled his hands from my face. "It isn't right. This isn't normal. It's not healthy."

"And what *is* normal, Amy? What's healthy?" He stepped back, crossing his arms over his chest. "Can you define it for me, please? Because I'd love to hear you describe this 'normal' and 'healthy' relationship and explain why ours doesn't qualify."

"We don't have a… relationship. You're blackmailing me into having sex with you. Everything between us is built on manipulation and coercion."

His eyes gleamed. "So you've hated every minute

of it, then? You've endured every orgasm I've given you under duress?"

I looked away. "You know I haven't. It's complicated."

"You're avoiding my question. Tell me what healthy is. Describe how a normal relationship works."

"I don't have to."

"No. You don't know *how to*," he contended. "So you'd rather throw away what we have, even though you want it, because you don't think it's what you *should* want."

He was making my head spin. "I don't need you to psychoanalyze me," I snapped, looking back at him. "I'm not one of your x-club 'patients' or some xeno that's addicted to you."

But I was. I totally was.

And he loved me.

No, don't go there.

His mouth tightened. "What if I sent you terrifying emails daily, warning you of all the perils lurking around every corner of the universe? Would that make our relationship feel more *normal* to you? Would that be healthy? If I ended every email and phone communication to you with 'stay safe' or 'be careful,' would that make you feel loved?"

"You're blackmailing me," I repeated the obvious.

"You can't build a relationship on a blackmail arrangement."

A hint of amusement lightened his gaze. "I thought ours was built on the foundation of being only children?"

"Vair, this isn't funny anymore."

"You're right." Annoyance flared in his mercurial dark eyes, along with another emotion I didn't want to acknowledge a Krinar capable of: hurt. "The fact that you still believe my blackmail ploy—believe I'd actually ever consider going through with sharing private video footage of us with the public is far from amusing for me."

"Ploy?" My eyes narrowed. "Do you mean to tell me—"

"Amy, like I explained before, your parents programmed you to respond to fear, to threats of danger and intimidation." His raised voice was sharp and angry, belying the nonchalant shrug of his shoulders. "Of course I capitalized on that, knowing it was the most expeditious means of getting you to come back to my club."

My mouth dropped open. "Capitalized on? That's just a fancier way of saying you took advantage."

"Precisely." He pointed an accusing finger at me. "And guess what? You've loved it. Inwardly, you've rejoiced in the fact that *I* took full responsibility and bore all the guilt for our arrangement, allowing you to indulge in what you considered inappropriate fantasies. No matter what we did, you knew you could place the blame squarely on me, and that made it okay for you."

"That's not true!"

"Amy." He gave me a drill sergeant look.

Oh, fine. "Whatever. So maybe I was into *some* of it. It doesn't matter. It doesn't change the fact that we're still not compatible. Hell, our species can't even procreate. Shalee told Jay that human and Krinar couples aren't able to have babies."

Vair tilted his head, the corner of his mouth kicking up into a smile that made my pulse jump. "No. None have. *Yet.*" His warm, dark gaze fell to my breasts. "Interesting that you've given it such thought when you want nothing to do with me and my manipulation and coercion."

He leaned forward, invading my space and caging me in as he planted a hand on either side of my hips atop the desk.

"So now you object to us being together because Krinar and humans have not yet been proven compatible for procreation?" His voice was low and throaty, his eyes intimate as he asked, "Are you saying you want children with me?"

I felt my cheeks go red. "No, that's not what I'm saying."

"There are countless human couples incapable of procreation. Does that make them incompatible?"

"Of course not. Stop twisting things. I'm merely pointing out that we're not even the same species—that we literally come from two different worlds."

"Yes, and we're not the first Krinar and human to pair off, Amy. And we certainly won't be the last."

I placed a hand against his chest as his head dipped closer, his nose a hair away from mine. My voice emerged breathy as I threw out the last obstacle I could think of. "But what about my parents, Vair? I'll never be able to explain this—*you*—to them."

He cupped my face in his hands again, tipping it up. "I've already thought of that, darling." His nose nuzzled mine. "Let's tell them I'm still blackmailing you, hmm?" I felt his smile against my lips as his touched mine softly.

"You're so sick," I whispered, kissing him back. When I pulled away to catch my breath, I told him truthfully, "They're going to absolutely hate you."

He nodded. "Well, I'm prepared to blackmail them directly, too, if necessary. Do you think the threat of a Costa Rican human labor camp will make the idea of an eight-hundred-and-forty-seven-year-old Krinar sex club owner more palatable to them as a son-in-law?"

I released a hysterical giggle and shook my head,

even as I cringed internally at how bad the description of my E.T. lover truly did and would sound to my parents.

"You really don't know my mother." I bit my lip. "I'm afraid this is going to require multiple phony YouTube videos about how much Ks enjoy the taste of human brains."

"Oh, and I'm the sick one?" he said with a laugh.

I shrugged.

"Well, darling… for you, I think it can be arranged."

Part Three

THE EXPOSÉ

CHAPTER THIRTY-ONE

Was this really happening?

I pinched myself. Discreetly, of course, but Vair—who noticed absolutely freaking *everything* about me—saw it, and a satyr-like grin tugged at the corners of his full, dangerously sexy mouth.

"Yes, it's real, little human," he whispered wickedly. "And I promise not to eat *them*—only you, okay?"

A violent blush crept up my neck. "Hush," I hissed, grabbing his hand and squeezing it with all my puny human strength. "They'll overhear."

We were standing in front of my parents' house in Skaneateles, where Vair and I were about to have dinner with my family for the first time. If it hadn't been for the Krinar nanocytes in my system, I'd have thought the heart palpitations I was having were a premature heart attack.

But according to Vair, I couldn't have a heart attack anymore. Or get any other human disease, which apparently included getting older. Now that I was officially Vair's charl, with proper nanocytes and all, I had immunity to *everything*, death from aging included.

I still hadn't fully processed that, and I didn't know if I would anytime soon. It was enough that I'd been dating Vair—full-on, actual dating—for the past two months, ever since he'd showed up in my office and bent me over my desk, fucking my brains out until I'd agreed to give this madness a go.

Not that Vair regarded what we're doing as "dating." In his eyes, we were simply together. Forever. He wasn't my *boyfriend*. Oh, no. That would be too straightforward and egalitarian. He was my *cheren*—which, if I understood that Krinar term right, meant that he basically owned my ass.

But in a loving, cherishing, forever-responsible-for-me kind of way.

I hadn't processed that part of it either, nor was I in any hurry to do so. Vair *acted* like my boyfriend—albeit of the stalking, recording-my-every-move, ridiculously possessive variety—and that was good enough for me. I continued to work at *The Herald*, where I'd finally gotten a couple of meaty assignments, and the rest of the time we spent together, going out to dinner at the best restaurants in the city, visiting parks and museums, and hanging out with Jay and his Krinar girlfriend Shalee (*she* had no problems with that label). That is, when we weren't having unhealthy amounts of mind-blowing, very non-vanilla sex either at Vair's obscenely luxurious penthouse or at his kinky "research facility"—a.k.a. the x-club.

"What made you decide to become a human behaviorist?" I'd asked him a few weeks ago over breakfast, after I'd woken up still exhausted from observing an all-night x-club orgy (while being fucked by Vair out of sight of the orgy participants, naturally). "No offense, but I wouldn't have pegged you for a scientist."

"Oh?" His eyebrows had arched. "What would you have pegged me for?"

"Oh, I don't know…" If these had been Victorian times, I'd have labeled him a high-society rake, but that was too silly to vocalize. "A *real* sex club owner?"

His teeth had flashed white as he'd picked up a strawberry. "I *am* a real sex club owner; there's nothing fake about my club. And as you know"—those teeth had sunk seductively into the plump berry—"I thoroughly enjoy the research we do there."

Ignoring my body's reaction to that statement, as well as my primal urge to lick the strawberry juice off his delicious bottom lip, I'd determinedly pressed ahead. "I'm serious, Vair. What made you decide to go into that profession? The first time we met, you said you'd been bored on Krina. Were you just messing around with me? Playing a part of the playboy Krinar suffering from ennui?"

He'd chuckled at that, but then his expression had grown more serious. "No, darling. I've never pretended to be anything other than what I am with you. I *had been* bored on Krina. Nothing really held my interest for long, so for most of my life, I'd been a dabbler, going from one field to another without truly finding myself or making any major contribution. It wasn't until our Council had decided to come to Earth that I discovered the poorly explored field of human behavior, and it became a passion of mine. That is, until *you* became a passion of mine, little human, irrational behavior and all."

I'd thrown a berry at him then, but more out of awkwardness at hearing again about his feelings than out of any real anger at being called "irrational."

Because I *was*.

I was crazy irrational when it came to him.

For one thing, though Vair often told me that he

loved me—or spouted off some variation of those words—I still hadn't mustered the courage to tell him how *I* felt. How even when we were in the middle of the kinkiest, dirtiest sex session, I was acutely aware of a growing undertone of tenderness between us, of a connection so deep it felt like it was embedded in my bone marrow. For whatever reason, I'd been keeping quiet about how I was starting to miss him when I was at work, even if I'd seen him that very morning, and how when we were apart, I checked my phone every minute, hoping to see a text from him.

A blush-inducing, horribly inappropriate text that would make me want to sink through the floor and orgasm at the same time.

It made me a coward, I was sure, but it had been so much easier when I'd regarded Vair as a villain. *When he'd been blackmailing me into doing what I wanted.*

And yes, I could admit that now. Unerringly, like the behaviorist that he was, Vair had found just the right approach to take with me. I had needed his implied threats to overcome the fears embedded in me by my parents, to fight my natural inclination to avoid all that was different and scary.

An inclination that I was still struggling with, to a small degree—hence my inability to admit to him how much I was beginning to need him.

How I was falling for him, despite my lingering fear of the unknown.

"You ready?" Vair asked, tugging me out of my parent-meeting-induced panicked musings. Grinning, he squeezed my hand back—but gently, so as not to crush my frail human bones. I must've still looked like I was about to throw up, though, because he raised my hand to his lips and dropped a gentle kiss on my knuckles. "It's going to be okay, darling, I promise. They'll love me. And if not, there are always those brain-eating videos on YouTube…"

I nodded, unconvinced, but it was too late.

Vair was already pressing on the doorbell.

CHAPTER THIRTY-TWO

It was a disaster.

I'd known it would be, of course, but Vair had insisted on this meeting, and here I was, cringing into my plate of overcooked broccoli as Mom stared at me with accusing, red-rimmed eyes and Dad alternated between stuttering out awkward questions about how long we'd been dating and drinking too much wine.

Partially, it was my fault. I'd kind of sprung Vair on my parents. While I'd been open about the fact that I had a new boyfriend, it had only been last night that I'd finally admitted the truth to my parents.

At 9:38 p.m., when Mom had called to double-check what time we'd be coming today, I'd fessed up that Vair was a K.

The hysterics that had followed were the worst I'd witnessed yet, and that was saying something.

"He's going to kill you! Murder you in your sleep!" Mom had sobbed into the phone while Dad had spammed my inbox with links to all the negative articles about Ks—some of them my own. "He's going to crack your skull and drain you of blood and—"

"I won't, I promise," Vair had interrupted, taking the phone from me, and that had set off a round of shrieking that must've been heard all the way to Alabama.

I'd repossessed the phone at that point and spent the next two-plus hours soothing my parents, telling them all about how well Vair treated me and how he never, ever ate human brains, not even when he was really hungry. After I'd finally hung up, I'd kept my phone next to me because I knew my mom—and sure enough, she'd called me six more times throughout the night, crying and begging me to leave and go get help, and why, oh why wouldn't the FBI listen to her insistence that I'd been kidnapped and send a SWAT team to retrieve me?

So yeah, that had been a fun night.

And here we were now, in my parents' house, with my mom having served the blandest, most unappetizing meal I'd ever seen her make. I suspected it was her version of "fuck you, evil K."

Maybe she was hoping that Vair would extrapolate the overboiled broccoli into a threat to overboil *him* if he ever hurt me?

I wasn't sure, but it was embarrassing either way.

"*Sorry*," I mouthed to Vair when my mom went with my dad into the kitchen to get us a refill of water and wine—to wash down the unpalatable food. "I don't know why they did this."

I gestured helplessly at the table, where in addition to the overcooked broccoli and undercooked potatoes, half-squished, ancient-looking grapes stood in a bowl—apparently to be eaten for dessert.

Vair's dark eyes glinted with amusement. "Don't worry, darling. It'll take more than a bad meal to scare me off."

So he'd interpreted my mom's actions the same way I had, though he didn't know she was normally a good cook who'd gamely risen to the challenge of a plant-based diet.

Unless...

I narrowed my eyes at him. "Is my parents' house bugged?" I half-hissed, half-whispered, gripping the table as I leaned closer. "Have you been watching them, too?"

Is that how he knew this was a bad meal and not my mom's usual dinner fare?

The amusement in his gaze deepened. "What do you think?"

Ugh. Of course. I felt a flare of outrage on my parents' behalf, but I didn't have a chance to express it because my mom returned, carrying two glasses of water—which she plopped on the table in front of us so hard that some liquid sloshed over the rim.

Dad was on her heels, carrying an open bottle of wine and a tray with a charred-looking brownie.

So there *was* dessert other than the unappetizing grapes.

"Thanks, Mom," I said, picking up my water to take a sip. Belatedly, it occurred to me that she might've spit in Vair's glass—or put something bad in his food, in general—but I shoved the thought aside.

Even if she had done something so awful, it wasn't like he'd get sick from it.

"So, Vair…" Dad said after downing another glass of wine. "What are your intentions toward our daughter?"

I closed my eyes and prayed for one of Vair's wall/floor-dissolving tricks, so I could sink into the hole and disappear.

"Well," Vair said, completely calmly, "I'm in love with your daughter, Mr. Myers, so I'm hoping for a long-term relationship with her."

I opened my lids a sliver and verified it.

Yep. Not even a hint of discomfort or embarrassment on that perfectly formed face of his, nor any of his usual mockery.

He looked sincere. *Earnest*. Like a Boy Scout hoping to win his Scoutmaster's approval.

And my dad was lapping it up, nodding like he was in total agreement.

My eyes opened wider as Mom spoke to Vair for the first time, her voice only slightly higher pitched than usual. "How would something like that work, exactly? You are a different *species*." She emphasized the last word, making it sound like something dirty.

"Yes, we are, but that doesn't matter," Vair said, giving her a carefully modulated smile. One that aimed to soothe and disarm. "I'm sure you'll remember a time in human history when people felt the same way about unions between different races."

My mom's freckled cheeks flushed. Despite living in a ninety-eight-percent-white area, she prided herself on being "blind" to race. "That's n-not…" she stuttered. "I mean, that's not the same *at all*."

"Why?" Vair said, his tone gentle. "If I love your daughter and she loves me, what's wrong with us being together?"

Mom stared at him, speechless for once, and I knew I was wearing the same expression—a dumbfounded, "deer in the headlights" look of illogical fear confronting irrefutable logic. My heart thudded dully in my chest, and my hand bunched into a fist under the table as his words sank in deep, bypassing the layers of bullshit I'd used as my defenses.

A Krinar and a human, in love. What was wrong with it, indeed?

Why was I fighting this so hard?

Why was I so scared to admit how I feel?

For a few long moments, no one said anything, the silence stretching until it felt like a string on the verge of breaking.

Then my dad cleared his throat. "Um… wine, anyone?"

"Don't mind if I do," Vair said easily, as if we were all friends here, and as Mom shakily extended her empty wine glass, holding it next to Vair's, I stared at my Krinar, knowing—*no, feeling*—the truth.

We might not be the same species, but he handled my parents like a boss.

~

It was late by the time we got home, but I felt wired instead of tired, all but buzzing with nervous energy.

"We did it. Can you believe we did it?" I babbled as Vair led me into his penthouse. I hadn't been able to shut up the entire ride home. "And oh my God, the expression on Mom's face when you invited them to New York for Thanksgiving… I bet they thought you were going to say 'Krina.' And then when Dad tasted that awful brownie and literally spit it out… Do you think Mom *actually* swapped the salt and the sugar, like she claimed she did by accident? As in, the full amount? I mean, it sure tasted like that, but that's extreme, even for her. And then—"

"Amy." Vair's dark eyes held a vaguely predatory expression as he stopped me by pressing a gentle finger to my lips. "Hush, darling."

My eyes opened wide as he followed that with his clothing-dissolving trick—with my clothes and his— and my throat went dry as I stared at the masculine perfection laid bare before me.

Would I ever get used to him?

Was it possible to get used to someone so gorgeous?

He was already hard, his magnificent cock curving up to his navel, every muscle on his large body chiseled with inhuman precision. But it was the look on his face that stole my breath—a mixture of dark lust and unabashed tenderness, of hunger and sheer adoration.

Leaning in, he framed my face with his large palms, and my insides clenched in anticipation as his lips brushed across mine... once, twice, and then again. His breath was warm and tasted faintly of wine, his tongue soft and slick as he delved into my mouth, tasting me, teasing me. My hands curved around his solid wrists, and my heart hammered in my ribcage as a hot flush spread over my skin and an empty ache bloomed low in my core.

I needed him to fuck me.

Now.

First, though, I needed to tell him something important—something that had weighed on me the entire ride home, making my nerves jingle and my mouth run non-stop.

Something I should've told him long ago but had been too chicken to admit.

Breathing shallowly, I broke the kiss and pulled away. "Vair..." Despite my resolve, my voice shook as I stared up at him, still holding his wrists as though I could possibly restrain him. "Vair, I..."

He held my gaze, the tenderness in his eyes intensifying. "Yes, darling?"

He knew. Of course he knew.

From the very beginning, he'd understood me—even better than I'd understood myself.

"I love you," I said, my voice steadying as my nervousness evaporated, replaced by a surge of pure, true feeling. "I love everything about you, Vair, and I want us to make a real go of this—no matter what my parents or anyone else thinks."

"Do you now?" he murmured, a slow, warm smile curving his sensuous lips, and as he reached for me again, bending his head to claim me with a voracious kiss, I knew that this was it.

In a New York City x-club, I'd found my other half.

A Krinar I loved with all my heart.

EPILOGUE

Six Years Later

"Are you ready?" Vair asked, squeezing my hand, and I nodded as I took a deep breath and did a quick self-check.

Was I about to throw up? *No.*

Faint? *Unlikely.*

Squeal like a teenager meeting her rock star idol? *Quite possibly.*

It couldn't be helped, though. In a minute, we were about to enter a virtual meeting with the Krinar-human couple whose tumultuous love story had recently riveted the population of two planets.

Korum and Mia.

The most powerful K on the Council and the human girl he'd *married*.

"They'll love you," Vair assured me. "Your

manuscript blew them away, and they know there's no one who'd do a better job with their story."

I gulped, trying to settle my wayward pulse—which insisted on hammering like a woodpecker in my throat.

I could do this. I could absolutely, definitely do this. So what if they were higher profile than any celebrities? Or that Korum had been the driving force behind the Ks' invasion of Earth?

Vair believed in me—enough to use all the goodwill his research had generated with the Krinar Council to get me this meeting—and I was no longer a newbie journalist. Over the past six years, I'd interviewed other highly placed Krinar, as well as human government officials and members of the Resistance. My articles, short stories, and exposés were widely acknowledged to be well researched and insightful, and my first nonfiction novel—the unusual love story of Emily Ross and her cheren, Zaron—was about to be published.

I was a freaking pro, and I had no reason to be nervous.

Other than the fact that this was the biggest journalistic coup ever.

Okay, then. "Let's do this," I said firmly, and as Vair grinned at me, the world turned into a blur.

Fighting dizziness, I closed my eyes, and when I

opened them, I was no longer in Vair's New York City penthouse.

"Amy Myers and Vair, I presume?" a tall, intimidatingly gorgeous Krinar with peculiar golden eyes said, staring at me from across a long, floating table.

My nerves settled as I felt myself slide into my journalistic persona. With a practiced glance, I took in the petite human girl at his side and the ivory-colored sunlit room we were virtually sitting in.

A room in Korum's house on Krina.

"That's right," I answered smoothly, inclining my head at the couple in a gesture of respect. I knew better than to attempt a handshake with a male K. Vair would be tempted to kill him on the spot. "And you must be Korum and Mia?"

"That's us," the girl said, beaming at me. Her eyes were startlingly blue against the backdrop of her dark, wildly curly hair, and her smile was utterly radiant in her delicately featured face. "We're so pleased to meet you, Amy. And Vair, of course."

A heavy arm slid around my waist, and I looked up to see Vair incline his head as he drawled, "A pleasure, to be sure."

I barely stopped myself from rolling my eyes. *Ks and their ridiculous possessiveness.* Korum was holding Mia anchored to his side as if she might otherwise run away, so of course Vair had to stake a similar claim on me. Never mind that this was supposed to be a serious interview, or that both Ks rationally knew that neither had an interest in the other's charl. Or that we were all here virtually, and our actual bodies were on different planets.

Their territorial instincts didn't give two hoots about rationality or reason.

"So, Korum," I said, focusing on the task at hand, "how about we start at the very beginning? How did you and Mia first meet?"

He looked at her, and I saw his starkly beautiful features soften. Not a lot, but just enough to convey what anyone who'd watched a recording of their lavish wedding already knew.

He'd blast apart entire galaxies for her.

"Do you want to do the honors, my sweet?" he asked softly, and she smiled up at him, her small face glowing.

"If you insist." Still smiling, she turned to me. "It's kind of a long story. I'm not sure it'll all fit into one book."

"If it doesn't, then I'll make it into two or three books," I assured her. "Whatever is needed."

And as the human girl launched into her story, I jotted down, *"The air was crisp and clear as Mia walked briskly down a winding path in Central Park..."*

SNEAK PEEKS

Thank you for reading Amy & Vair's story! We hope you enjoyed it and would consider leaving a review.

Want to read more sizzling hot romance? Check out ***Just Like Animals***, a steamy standalone in Hettie Ivers's *Werelock Evolution* series, and ***Mia & Korum***, Anna Zaires's Krinar trilogy that started it all. To be notified of new releases, sign up for our newsletters at hettieivers.com and annazaires.com!

Want more Krinar hotness? Check out:

- ***The Krinar Captive*** – Emily & Zaron's full-length standalone romance, set just before the Invasion

- *Swept Away* – a short novella about Arus and Delia's meeting in Ancient Greece
- **The Krinar World stories** – Krinar romances written by other amazing authors

Love the dark side of romance? Grab these twisted sizzlers by Anna Zaires:

- *The Twist Me Trilogy* – an epic kidnapping romance featuring Nora & Julian
- *The Capture Me Trilogy* – Lucas & Yulia's enemies-to-lovers captive romance
- *Tormentor Mine* – Peter & Sara's tale of love, obsession, and revenge

Prefer action and sci-fi? Grab these collaborations with Dima Zales, Anna's hubby:

- *The Girl Who Sees* – the thrilling tale of Sasha Urban, a stage illusionist who discovers unexpected secret powers
- *Mind Dimensions* – the action-packed urban fantasy adventures of Darren, who can stop time and read minds
- *Transcendence* – the mind-blowing technothriller featuring venture capitalist

Mike Cohen, whose Braincocyte technology will forever change the world
- ***The Last Humans*** – the futuristic sci-fi/dystopian story of Theo, who lives in a world where nothing is as it seems
- ***The Sorcery Code*** – the epic fantasy adventures of sorcerer Blaise and his creation, the beautiful and powerful Gala

Love audiobooks? All Anna Zaires and Dima Zales titles are in audio. Visit annazaires.com to learn more!

And now please turn the page for a little taste of Anna Zaires's *Tormentor Mine*.

EXCERPT FROM TORMENTOR MINE

He came to me in the night, a cruel, darkly handsome stranger from the most dangerous corners of Russia. He tormented me and destroyed me, ripping apart my world in his quest for vengeance.

Now he's back, but he's no longer after my secrets.

The man who stars in my nightmares wants me.

"Are you going to kill me?"

She's trying—and failing—to keep her voice steady. Still, I admire her attempt at composure. I approached her in public to make her feel safer, but she's too smart to fall for that. If they've told her anything about my background, she must realize I can snap her neck faster than she can scream for help.

"No," I answer, leaning closer as a louder song comes on. "I'm not going to kill you."

"Then what do you want from me?"

She's shaking in my hold, and something about that both intrigues and disturbs me. I don't want her to be afraid of me, but at the same time, I like having her at my mercy. Her fear calls to the predator within me, turning my desire for her into something darker.

She's captured prey, soft and sweet and mine to devour.

Bending my head, I bury my nose in her fragrant hair and murmur into her ear, "Meet me at the Starbucks near your house at noon tomorrow, and we'll talk there. I'll tell you whatever you want to know."

I pull back, and she stares at me, her eyes huge in her pale face. I know what she's thinking, so I lean in again, dipping my head so my mouth is next to her ear.

"If you contact the FBI, they'll try to hide you from me. Just like they tried to hide your husband and the others on my list. They'll uproot you, take you away from your parents and your career, and it will all be for nothing. I'll find you, no matter where

EXCERPT FROM TORMENTOR MINE

you go, Sara… no matter what they do to keep you from me." My lips brush against the rim of her ear, and I feel her breath hitch. "Alternatively, they might want to use you as bait. If that's the case—if they set a trap for me—I'll know, and our next meeting won't be over coffee."

She shudders, and I drag in a deep breath, inhaling her delicate scent one last time before releasing her.

Stepping back, I melt into the crowd and message Anton to get the crew into positions.

I have to make sure she gets home safe and sound, unmolested by anyone but me.

∼

Order your copy of *Tormentor Mine* today!

ABOUT THE AUTHORS

Anna Zaires is a *New York Times, USA Today,* and #1 international bestselling author of sci-fi romance and contemporary dark erotic romance. She fell in love with books at the age of five, when her grandmother taught her to read. Since then, she has always lived partially in a fantasy world where the only limits were those of her imagination. Currently residing in Florida, Anna is happily married to Dima Zales (a science fiction and fantasy author) and closely collaborates with him on all their works.

To learn more, please visit www.annazaires.com.

Hettie Ivers is an accidental romance author who likes to escape the stress of her work week with a good dirty book—preferably one that's also funny.

Her current career does not allow much time for creative smut writing, but she loves to write after hours and on weekends and strives to publish one to two books per year, as life permits.

To learn more about Hettie and the books she has written, please feel free to visit her website at www.hettieivers.com, sign up for her newsletter, friend her on Facebook, or join her Facebook group to keep in touch.

Printed in Great Britain
by Amazon